He had an unsettling effect on her—like no one she'd ever met

He was so damn self-contained, yet below the surface she could sense his mind working. An aura of danger surrounded him that she couldn't quite resist.

Too bad he was the sexiest man she'd met in a long time. That was another major problem. He made her feel hot and needy, just by the way he looked at her.

And she knew that he found her attractive. That was part of the lure of the man for her—the exhilaration of knowing that he was responding to her…even in her condition.

Her lips firmed. She should be focused on the baby, not on this cowboy who had mysteriously stepped into her life.

USA TODAY Bestselling Author

REBECCA YORK

RUTH GLICK WRITING AS REBECCA YORK

RILEY'S RETRIBUTION

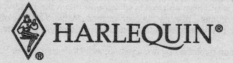

TORONTO • NEW YORK • LONDON
AMSTERDAM • PARIS • SYDNEY • HAMBURG
STOCKHOLM • ATHENS • TOKYO • MILAN • MADRID
PRAGUE • WARSAW • BUDAPEST • AUCKLAND

Special thanks and acknowledgment are given to Rebecca York for her contribution to the BIG SKY BOUNTY HUNTERS series.

ISBN 0-373-88659-4

RILEY'S RETRIBUTION

ABOUT THE AUTHOR

Award-winning, bestselling novelist Ruth Glick, who writes as Rebecca York, is the author of close to eighty books, including her popular 43 Light Street series for Harlequin Intrigue. Ruth says she has the best job in the world. Not only does she get paid for telling stories, she's also the author of twelve cookbooks. Ruth and her husband, Norman, travel frequently, researching locales for her novels and searching out new dishes for her cookbooks.

Books by Rebecca York

HARLEQUIN INTRIGUE

143—LIFE LINE*
155—SHATTERED VOWS*
167—WHISPERS IN THE NIGHT*
179—ONLY SKIN DEEP*
188—BAYOU MOON
193—TRIAL BY FIRE*
213—HOPSCOTCH*
233—CRADLE AND ALL*
253—WHAT CHILD IS THIS?*
273—MIDNIGHT KISS*
289—TANGLED VOWS*
298—TALONS OF THE FALCON†
301—FLIGHT OF THE RAVEN†
305—IN SEARCH OF THE DOVE†
318—TILL DEATH US DO PART*
338—PRINCE OF TIME*
407—FOR YOUR EYES ONLY*
437—FATHER AND CHILD*
473—NOWHERE MAN*
500—SHATTERED LULLABY*
525—AFTER DARK
        "Counterfeit Wife"
534—MIDNIGHT CALLER*
558—NEVER TOO LATE*

606—BAYOU BLOOD BROTHERS
        "Tyler"
625—THE MAN FROM TEXAS**
633—NEVER ALONE**
641—LASSITER'S LAW**
667—FROM THE SHADOWS*
684—GYPSY MAGIC
        "Alessandra"
706—PHANTOM LOVER*
717—INTIMATE STRANGERS*
745—THE BOYS IN BLUE
        "Jordan"
765—OUT OF NOWHERE*
783—UNDERCOVER ENCOUNTER
828—SPELLBOUND
885—RILEY'S RETRIBUTION

*43 Light Street
**43 Light Street/Mine To Keep
†Peregrine Connection

CAST OF CHARACTERS

Riley Watson—He was known as the chameleon, but could he pull off the charade of his life?

Courtney Rogers—Was she an innocent bystander, or was she working with the terrorists?

Jake Bradley—He hated Riley for reasons no one knew.

Kelly Manning—Was he loyal to Courtney, or did he have another agenda?

Cameron Murphy—Would the leader of Big Sky get his bounty?

Boone Fowler—Why was he hiding out on a ranch in Montana?

Greg Nichols—What exactly happened after Courtney fired him?

Sheriff Bobby Pennington—He stood for law and order in Spur City...or did he?

Prince Nikolai of Lukinburg—He claimed to have good reasons for coming to Montana. But a hidden agenda lurked just beyond the fringes of his policy.

Chapter One

Even the weather was fighting her, Courtney Rogers thought as she pulled the pickup truck out of a skid on the two-lane highway.

If she'd known this freak storm was blowing up like a nasty surprise from the gods of the north, she never would have gone into Spur City.

"No, be honest. You would have left at five in the morning to beat the storm," she muttered.

Since Ernie Hastings, her damn unreliable ranch manager, had quit six weeks ago, she'd been too short of help to send anyone else for food and other supplies. And too short of money to leave the buying to someone who might choose sugar cereal instead of oatmeal.

Only, the trip into town hadn't quite turned out the way she'd expected. Midge Buckley had walked rapidly in the other direction when she'd seen Courtney coming, and Jeb Bittner at the general store had given her a hard time—just for the heck of it.

"Well, I guess you never really know your neighbors," she muttered, then switched on the radio.

An antique Hank Williams song filled the cab. Unfortunately, it was the wrong choice, since old Hank was singing about lost love, and she couldn't stop herself from reacting to the sadness of the lyrics.

When her vision blurred, she blinked her eyes.

"Get a grip," she ordered herself. "You've come through bad times before. You'll do it again."

The swirling flakes and another recent snowfall hid the craggy Montana landscape, but she knew this stretch of road as well as she knew the vegetable garden in back of the ranch house.

She'd been born and raised in this country, and she'd been traveling back and forth to Spur City since her mom had strapped her into an infant car seat for the trip.

The Golden Saddle horse farm where she lived was a legacy from her parents. Mom had died five years ago. Dad had lived three years longer. And she'd been back home for the past two years— while her marriage was coming apart at the seams.

Her own lost love. Buried under a clash of lifestyles and values. And finally...buried for good.

She didn't want to think about that. She'd loved

Edward Rogers, even when she'd told him it was all over between them.

But she'd still prayed they could work things out. And after their divorce, her former husband had come to see her one last time before shipping out to an overseas assignment in Lukinburg.

Could they have made the out-of-kilter relationship work? She didn't know. Because Lieutenant Edward Rogers hadn't come home alive. He'd left her with a load of guilt and...

She tightened her hands on the wheel.

"Like Daddy always said, there's no use crying over spilled milk. You've got to clean up the mess and go on from there."

All she could do was go forward and try to dig herself out of the mess that had become her life.

Maybe her new ranch manager, Riley Watson, would make a difference.

And maybe he'd be just another piece of bad news.

Up ahead, the road crossed under a bridge, and she squinted because she thought she saw a figure on the span above her—just visible through the whirlpool of flakes.

A man was looking toward her. She couldn't see him very well, but his posture looked strangely rigid...as if someone had fashioned him out of ice.

She squinted into the storm, trying to work out

what the guy was doing out here in the middle of nowhere. Was he in trouble and looking for help from a passing motorist down here on the highway?

If so, she felt obligated to stop, because in this open country he could freeze to death if his vehicle had broken down.

She slowed, still dividing her attention between the man and the highway. Come to think of it, she didn't see a vehicle. Had he walked to the bridge from farther down the highway?

As she squinted up at him, he moved. She blinked, trying to figure out what she was seeing. It looked as if he'd raised a rifle to his shoulder and was aiming it down toward her.

There was no other car or truck on the road.

If that guy was really planning to shoot at someone—it was her.

"No," she whispered into the silence of the car.

Her heart was thumping as she sped up, trying to swerve out of the way or make it under the bridge before he could fire.

But she was too late. A rifle shot cracked. And the slug tore into the glass just above her head and to the right.

It was as though a stone had hit the windshield. Only that was no stone.

She skidded on the snow-covered road, skidded

under the bridge, then kept barreling forward. Fighting the wheel, she managed to keep from crashing into the concrete abutment on her right. Defensive driving lessons her dad had given her leaped into her mind, and she pumped the brakes to slow her speed. But she still wasn't able to control the truck. When she shot out from under the bridge, she was heading toward the shoulder.

Her hands were clenched on the wheel as she plunged off the snow-covered blacktop, crunched across the gravel and into a field.

Lord knew what was under the snow. The truck swayed, and she fought to keep the vehicle from turning over.

Probably her efforts had little to do with the eventual outcome, but she came to a stop against something solid she couldn't see. Probably a rock.

Quickly she cut the engine. Still clutching the wheel, she struggled to bring her breathing back to normal as she fought a terrible sense of dread.

"Think rationally," she ordered herself. "Going into panic mode won't do you any good."

One by one, she gathered her mental resources. Then, slowly and deliberately, she took a physical inventory. She felt no sudden pains. And when she moved her arms and legs, they worked. With shaky fingers, she unbuttoned her coat and reached inside to press her hand against her middle. Everything seemed to be okay—no thanks to the guy up on the bridge.

Oh, Lord—the guy on the bridge! She'd forgotten about him for a moment. Would he come down here to finish her off? Or was hitting her pickup enough?

With a jerky motion she reached for the gun that she kept in the compartment of the truck door.

Seconds ticked by. Then minutes. And she began to relax a little. It looked as if the shooter had turned tail and run.

But she was still in big trouble. The windshield was a maze of cracks, the temperature was below zero, and the snow was going to bury her truck in no time flat.

With her gun across her lap and one eye cocked toward the road, she picked up the cell phone from the seat beside her and tried to make a call.

Reception out here was never great, and the snow didn't help. All she got was a notice on the screen that the service couldn't make the connection.

"Oh, sugar," she muttered, slapping the phone down and peering outside.

Despite the dire circumstances, she grinned. Her campaign to improve her language was working. She'd reached for a curse and managed to say "oh, sugar" instead of something stronger.

After waiting several minutes to make sure she

wasn't being stalked, she tried to turn the motor on again. But the truck wouldn't start. Which meant she couldn't run the heater. And she could already feel the cold creeping inside the cab.

She peered out the window, thinking about her limited options.

She could try to walk, which wouldn't get her far in this weather. Or she could stay put and hope someone found her—and not the guy up on the bridge who had pulled the trigger.

Neither choice was good. But she figured that staying in the truck offered the best chance of survival.

THE SMOTHERING CLOUD OF SNOW swirling out of the sky was disorienting, Riley Watson thought as he drove toward the Golden Saddle Ranch. In fact, everything about this assignment was disorienting.

Three weeks ago he'd been working as part of a team—the Big Sky Bounty Hunters. With Bryce Martin, Jacob Powell, Aidan Campbell, Joseph Brown and the rest. Now he was all alone on a Montana highway in the middle of a blizzard—and fighting a feeling of unreality.

He swallowed hard. Too bad an explosion had changed everything.

But he knew it had been Big Sky's best option.

After escaping from Boone Fowler's torture camp on Devil's Fork Island, they'd pulled off a pretty nifty charade. As far as the world—and the bad guys—knew, everybody on the team, including himself, had been blown to smithereens.

The rest of the men were lying low, waiting for Riley's signal to come out of hiding.

Like a slippery eel, Fowler had slithered away. But Big Sky had pinpointed his location. He had rented some unused buildings on the Golden Saddle Ranch and reconstituted his gang as the Montana Militia for a Free America, a supposedly law-abiding group of men who only wanted to defend themselves against the forces of big government. There were other similar groups out here—which made the cover story all too plausible.

So why had ranch owner, Courtney Rogers, given Fowler a place to stay? Was she a pal of his? Was she working for a terrorist organization? Or was she an innocent bystander caught in the middle of a bad situation?

Big Sky couldn't simply drive up to her front door, ask some pointed questions and expect straight answers. So Colonel Cameron Murphy, their leader, had devised a plan to put Riley onto the ranch where he could find out what Fowler was up to and what role Ms. Rogers was playing in the game.

Privately, Riley didn't much like the scenario, because it could put an innocent woman in jeopardy.

If she was really innocent. He'd pored over the information they'd given him about her, trying to figure her out. She was twenty-eight. She'd been born out here in the middle of nowhere and lived all her life on the Golden Saddle—except for four years at the university, then a year in Billings after she'd gotten married. But she'd come home to the ranch when her husband had taken an overseas assignment. And her marriage had been rocky after that.

She was a rancher at heart. As a girl, she'd won a bunch of blue ribbons with her 4-H projects. And she could rope and ride, shoot and tend the stock with the best of the guys. As far as he could see, she was happy in this patch of Montana.

But Edward Rogers couldn't stay put in one place. He liked travel—and danger. Which was how she'd ended up a widow.

And now Big Sky was messing with her life. For starters, they had paid Rogers's ranch manager, Ernie Hastings, a large sum of money to walk out on her. Then Riley had applied for the job. His fake résumé had looked good in the e-mails he and Mrs. Rogers had exchanged. This afternoon, he was on the way to the ranch for a face-to-face interview.

His nerves were jumping. But he kept reminding himself why the colonel had picked him. He'd grown up on a ranch in Texas, so he had the skills to play the role Big Sky had assigned him.

Another point in his favor was Courtney Rogers's situation. She was shorthanded. Her father had left the ranch in debt. And her former husband wasn't coming to her rescue, because he'd gotten himself killed during an assignment in Lukinburg.

As Riley drove toward the Golden Saddle, his thoughts shifted from the ranch owner to Boone Fowler, and his stomach clenched.

He'd been trying not to dwell on that part of the assignment. The last time he'd seen the militia leader, Riley had been Fowler's prisoner. Thank God he'd been in disguise. And working under an assumed name—Craig O'Riley. When they'd captured him, his hair had been long and dyed dark. Then his captors had shaved his head with a dull razor. Lucky for him, his hair was thick enough to hide the scars.

Not that he was vain enough to worry about some razor nicks on his skull spoiling his appearance. But they could have interfered with one of his biggest assets as a bounty hunter—his ability to fool his quarry into thinking he was some-one else.

Among the men of Big Sky, he was known as the chameleon. For him, changing his appearance was as natural to him as changing his shirt.

Ironically, this time, he was going as himself, with sun-streaked brown hair, hazel eyes and a confident bearing he wasn't exactly feeling. But that last part was even more important than the physical attributes. He had to convince Boone Fowler that they were equals—not former pris-oner and captor. Because if Fowler cottoned on to his real identity, he was a dead man.

The stakes were too high for failure. And not just the personal stakes. Since their captivity, Big Sky had discovered that Fowler's militia wasn't working alone. It seemed they were tied to a ter-rorist movement bent on influencing American policy on Lukinburg. And the terrorists were prob-ably in league with the former King Aleksandr Petrov—who wanted to keep his ass on the throne.

So Riley's ultimate goal was to find out what Boone Fowler was up to, then contact Big Sky so they could scoop up him and his men and collect their bounty.

Nothing much, he thought with a laugh.

But first he had to convince Courtney Rogers

to hire him so he could find out what side she was really on.

As he drove through the snow, a shape loomed above and slightly ahead of him. Uncertain of what he was seeing, he slowed.

When he drew closer, the shape resolved itself into a bridge.

The snow poured down from the sky like someone was up there emptying buckets of the stuff. But the bridge presented a man-made roof.

Once he drove into the shelter of the span, he saw something interesting—a set of skid marks on the sheltered blacktop. Obviously a vehicle had come shooting into the underpass, with the driver barely in control.

Then what?

Inching forward, he followed the trail. It emerged from the overhang and into the swirl of snow. The white stuff had almost obliterated the tire tracks on the other side, but he could follow their path as they skidded toward the right.

When he projected the trajectory to its logical conclusion, he saw a green pickup truck that had taken a header into a field.

So, had somebody rescued the driver? Or was he still inside?

Riley slowed, then pulled onto the shoulder and ahead of the vehicle.

When he climbed out, the first thing he saw was that the windshield of the truck was crazed. Maybe a rock had spun up from the road—causing a one-car accident.

Shivering in a sudden blast of cold, he was glad to be wearing a heavy shearling coat, a Western hat, boots and gloves.

The snow was up to his boot tops, making the shoulder surface slippery, and he walked carefully as he started back the way he'd come—his eyes trained on the truck.

He'd been thinking nobody was inside. Now he revised his assumption since he saw no footprints around the driver's door and the windows were fogged. He couldn't see much, but he did detect the vague outline of a figure behind the wheel.

He cupped his hands around his mouth as he approached. "You okay?"

Nobody answered, so he reached for the handle and pulled the door open.

Several impressions registered at once. The person inside the cab was small. A small man—no, a woman.

Her features, what he could see of them, were definitely feminine. Large camel-colored eyes. A delicate nose. Nicely shaped lips. A bit of reddish-brown hair poking from below her wool ski cap.

She was wearing a man's heavy coat and a wool

scarf. For further protection against the cold, she had wrapped a blanket around her legs. But the blanket wasn't the main detail that smacked him in the face.

The woman held an old-fashioned, long-barreled revolver in her right hand, and it was pointed directly at his chest.

The weapon might be old, but it looked to be in excellent shape.

"Get away from me, you bastard," she ordered in a shaky voice, "or I'll kill you."

Chapter Two

Riley raised his hands to shoulder level, gloved palms outward, thinking he was in deep swamp water now. Make that freezing swamp water.

He hadn't expected an attack when he opened the door. So he hadn't drawn his own weapon. It was a SIG-Sauer P-226—not the standard issue with Western wear. But he'd figured that enough guys carried them around here that he could get away with it.

"Put away the six-shooter. I came to help you."

"Sure," she answered. "That's why you shot at me." Her words were slurred, her face was pale, and he knew in that dangerous moment that she was suffering from hypothermia. She wasn't thinking clearly, and she could shoot him if he blinked—or if he took a step back. On the other hand, if he stood here with snow swirling around him and tried to keep talking to her, she could drift dangerously close to death.

"Let me help you," he said calmly.

"Get away." Just the effort to talk seemed to be draining her remaining energy.

"Don't do anything foolish," he answered, edging closer. When the pistol wavered, he made his move, diving for her gun hand, pointing the weapon toward the floor even as he wrestled the gun away from her.

She had the strength of desperation, and she wasn't willing to give up easily. As she fought him, he kept imagining disaster—one or the other of them with a gaping bullet wound turning the snow crimson.

It felt like centuries as he fought her for the gun, trying to keep either one of them from getting hurt. Probably it was only seconds.

She moaned as he twisted the weapon from her grasp. To hide it from sight, he set it on the ground below the truck.

"Oh, sugar." She said it like a curse, and he found the combination of vehemence and ladylike language oddly endearing.

"It's all right. Everything's going to be all right," he murmured as he cupped one gloved hand over her shoulder.

Tears welled in her eyes, yet he saw her struggling for control. In the next moment, he found that letting his guard down was a big mistake.

Still on the offensive, she made her gloved hands into small fists, pounding against his chest and shoulders.

"Hey, cut it out," he growled. "There's only so far I'm willing to carry chivalry."

The situation was still deteriorating, and he couldn't help wondering which one of them was going to end up getting hurt.

Luckily, the hypothermia had sapped the little wildcat's strength, and he was able to lean into the cab and wrap his arms around her, drawing her close.

"Honey?" she said.

Before he could answer, she whispered, "You came back to help me." Whoever her honey was, he had a calming effect on the woman.

She let her head drop to his shoulder, and he cradled her against his body, thinking she felt delicate and feminine under the heavy coat she wore. Holding her was no hardship.

Her hands came up again, and he braced for an attack. But she only opened one of the buttons on his coat and slipped her gloved hand inside. When her fingers flattened against his shirtfront, he felt his heart thunk. Then she turned her face and stroked her lips against his cheek.

Easing away, he looked into her sleepy camel-colored eyes. "We need to warm you up," he muttered.

"Oh, yeah," she answered in a voice that had gone from panicked to sultry.

He'd climbed out of his SUV to rescue a stranded driver, and he'd expected to be greeted with relief when he opened the truck door. Instead she'd fought like a wounded tiger. Now she was coming on to him—and she probably didn't even realize what she was doing.

Keeping his voice even, he said, "I think you've mistaken me for someone else. I saw you on the road and figured you needed help."

He watched her pull herself together and focus on him. Maybe she was really seeing him for the first time. In any event, her expression went from sexy to sharp in the blink of an eye.

"If you're here to help me, why did you take a potshot at me?"

"I didn't shoot at you," he said, hoping he was putting the right amount of sincerity into his voice.

"Oh, yeah? If you're on the level, then go away and leave me alone."

He struggled to rein in his exasperation. "It's too cold for that. Just for a minute, try to think logically. If I'd wanted to kill you, I could already have done it."

Either the reasoning had sunk in, or she was too exhausted to keep up the struggle because he saw her shoulders sag.

He picked up her gun from the ground and shoved it into his belt. Then he reached for the lady.

"What the hell are you doing?"

"Getting you out of the cold."

She was back in fighting mode, kicking against him, and he ignored the thuds from her Western boots as he carried her back to the SUV, set her in the passenger seat and slammed the door before hurrying around to the driver's side. To his chagrin, he almost lost his balance.

As he climbed behind the wheel, she was already reaching for the door handle,

He yanked her hand away. "Don't do anything foolish. Let me get you out of this storm."

She gave a sigh and leaned back against the seat as though admitting defeat.

But he wasn't going to trust that. Not hardly. She was too far out of it—and too determined to fight him.

He tucked the blanket more firmly around her and fastened her seat belt, wishing he'd feel her shiver. That would be a good sign.

After starting the car, he turned up the heat and drove slowly down the road, squinting into a swirl of white and wondering how far he'd have to go before he found both of them shelter.

After twenty minutes, he spotted a red-and-blue neon sign just visible through the driving snow.

Leaning forward, he struggled to make out the words. Finally he saw Buckskin Motel. Vacancy.

"Thank God," he murmured, then looked toward his passenger. She was sitting with her eyes closed, breathing slowly and evenly.

Was it safe to leave her?

He thought about the scene in the lobby if he showed up carrying her over his shoulder like a caveman dragging his mate off to make love. No. Better leave her in the car—unless she was going to make a run for it.

Wondering how fast he could get in and out, he pulled up beside the office door and cut the engine. Next to the office was a small restaurant. All the comforts of home.

"Do us both a favor and stay put, sugar," he ordered, then quickly exited the SUV and dashed into the lobby.

"I need a room to wait out the storm, and maybe something to eat later," he told the old man who came through a door in response to the tinkling bell over the door.

"You're in luck. We've got a few rooms left. And Molly just made a big pot of her beef and vegetable soup."

"I may try some," Riley allowed. He kept one eye on his SUV while he filled out the form and paid with a credit card. His passenger didn't move. And he felt reluctant to talk about her to the man behind the counter.

She'd said someone had shot at her, and she had a serious hole in her windshield. What if it wasn't a stone that had done the damage? And what if the shooter was looking for her—and somebody talking about her led the bad guys to this motel?

He put long odds on that scenario. But in his years with the Special Forces and then with Big Sky, he'd learned caution. So he decided to keep her under wraps, so to speak, until he could have a coherent conversation with her.

Completing the transaction as quickly as possible, he hurried back to the SUV, then drove down the row of motel rooms and around the back where the old guy had directed him.

When he came around to the passenger door, the woman stirred. "What?"

"You can't stay in the car. I'm no medic, but I know what you need. I've got to get you inside where it's warm and cozy."

She roused herself enough to slit her eyes and ask, "Are we at the ranch?"

"No, a motel."

Her eyes blinked fully open, and she focused on him again—obviously seeing a man she didn't know and didn't trust. "I'm not going into any motel room with you."

"If I had wanted to try anything funny, I could have done that in the car."

Before she could object, he stepped away from the vehicle and unlocked the motel room door. Returning to the SUV, he scooped her up and carried her inside, where he laid her on the bed.

After bringing in a few things, he closed and locked the door, then fired up the heating unit under the window and put her gun in a drawer so she couldn't grab it and shoot him. When he turned back to the woman on the bed, he saw that she was dozing again.

The thought crossed his mind that a warm bath might be just what she needed. It made sense in medical terms, but he canceled that plan as soon as it surfaced. No way was he going to do anything that intimate.

But he did pull off her boots, gloves, hat and jacket, tossing them in the general direction of the chair in the corner. Leaving the rest of her clothing on, he bundled her under the covers.

"Can you tell me your name?" he asked.

"No."

Because she couldn't remember? Or because she didn't want to?

He hadn't seen a purse in the truck. Maybe he'd missed it. She might have a wallet on her, but he didn't think it was a good idea to pat her down.

She spoke again, her voice faint and urgent. "Honey?"

Apparently, she wanted them back on intimate terms again.

"I'm not your man," he answered, looking at the mass of rich chestnut hair that had been hidden under her hat. The cloud of hair around her face totally changed her appearance, making her look feminine and seductive. But he didn't have much time to study her, because she was speaking again, and her tone had turned high and urgent. "I need you to hold me. Please."

She was calling out to another guy. But she sounded on the edge of panic. When she pushed the covers aside and swung her legs out of bed, he figured he'd better act before she exited the room into the cold and snow again.

"Come on, sugar, let's get back into bed and get you nice and warm." He kicked his own boots off and shrugged out of his coat.

Leaving his jeans and shirt on, he climbed into bed and gathered her to him, then pulled the blankets up around them and held her close, stroking her hair and shoulders, murmuring low, reassuring words.

Apparently he had calmed her fears because she closed her eyes and snuggled against him, burying her face in his shirt so that all he could see was her shining mass of chestnut hair.

Very appealing hair, with a strawberry scent that must have come from her shampoo.

"It's been so long," she murmured.

"Mmm-hmm."

When she started to shiver, he figured she was warming up. She was going to be okay, and maybe he should let her go.

But he was enjoying holding her. She was soft and relaxed in his arms, and he hadn't been in bed with a woman since forever; to be exact, not since before the damn prison camp. After getting out of that hellhole, he'd felt too needy, and he hadn't wanted to inflict his insecurities on some random woman he picked up in a bar.

So he and Miss Sugar might as well share a little counterfeit intimacy. And when she realized he wasn't her lover, they'd deal with the consequences. All that sounded logical. But he wondered how clearly he was thinking himself as he stroked his lips against that beautiful, sweet-smelling hair.

Who was she? What was she doing out on the road? Had someone really shot at her?

She was talking again, her voice still dreamy. Apparently addressing herself to her man, she said, "You came back, and there's something I have to tell you." She swallowed. "But I know you're not going to like it."

His muscles tensed as he prepared to hear some other guy's bad news. "What do you want to tell me?" he managed to say.

She didn't answer, and he saw to his profound relief that she had drifted into sleep again. Which postponed the inevitable confrontation.

He was exhausted, too. From the long ride through the driving snow. From fighting her. And from all the sleepless nights when he'd contemplated this assignment.

To be brutally honest, he'd hated being the lucky sucker assigned to cozy up to Boone Fowler—after being beaten and tortured in the guy's prison camp. But he hadn't tried to duck the job, because somebody had to do it…and he was better equipped than most. He'd always talked a good game, and he looked nothing like Fowler's former prisoner. And he was pretty sure he knew the right buttons to push to talk his way into the militia leader's organization.

He hoped.

He raised his head and looked at the woman next to him. She was sleeping normally.

Probably, he shouldn't leave her alone. But that didn't mean he had to stay in bed with her, either. He should crawl out from under the covers and try to sleep on the chair in the corner. In a minute, he thought. He'd just relax here for a little while before he heaved himself out of this nice soft bed.

His eyelids drifted closed, then snapped open again. Lying in bed with this woman was wrong, not to mention dangerous. She could wake up and strangle him.

Not likely, he told himself. He wasn't going to sleep. He was only going to rest for a few minutes. Then he'd get up. It was a reasonable scenario. But he drifted off before he could put the plan into action.

COURTNEY'S EYES BLINKED open. For a moment she had no idea where she was, and panic choked off her breath.

Had Eddie brought her here?

She remembered talking to him just a few minutes ago.

No. That was impossible. Eddie was dead. The man next to her in bed definitely wasn't him. She knew that for sure.

Memories floated at the edge of her consciousness, and she struggled to grasp them. When she did, they brought back a mixture of embarrassment and panic.

Someone up on the bridge had shot at her. She'd tried to get away, skidded off the road and been stuck in the truck—until this man had come along.

She'd tried to shoot him. But he'd overpowered her and driven her—where?

She looked around cautiously and didn't see her gun.

She turned her face toward the man on the bed.

He was a handsome devil with sun-streaked brown hair, long lashes, high cheekbones and sensual lips.

Of course, his appearance didn't mean squat. Underneath those good looks, he could still be a snake. Could she find the gun without waking him? Probably not.

The place looked like a motel room. If this guy was out to help her, why hadn't they gone to the ranch?

Presumably, because she hadn't told him who she was.

Vaguely she remembered his asking her name and her refusing to give it. That might be a dream, though. Like the part about Eddie.

But she couldn't remember all the details. Her most vivid impression was that she'd been chilled to the bone—and out of her mind.

The man next to her moved, and her body went rigid.

"I won't hurt you," he said, shifting so that he could meet her panicked gaze.

"Who are you?"

"Riley Watson."

As the full impact of the situation hit her, she moaned. "Oh, Lord."

"And you are?" he prompted.

"Courtney Rogers."

His complexion went gray, and he was out of bed and halfway across the room before she could blink. "Sorry, ma'am. Wrong bed."

They stared at each other across eight feet of charged space.

"You are the Riley Watson who applied for a job at the Golden Saddle Ranch?" she clarified, knowing she must sound like an idiot. How many other guys named Riley Watson would there be in this part of Montana?

"Yes, ma'am."

"It's not going to work out. I can't hire you."

He stood up straighter. "Why? Because I stopped you from shooting me?"

She felt her face heat.

"Or because I got into bed with you?"

"That part."

"You were calling me honey. You were half out of it, and you asked me to hold you."

"So you took advantage of me."

"Took advantage?" he sputtered. "You've still got all your clothes on, haven't you?"

She watched him consider how that must have sounded.

"And you needed me to help warm you up," he added, then looked as if he wished he hadn't stuck his foot further into his mouth.

She honestly hadn't remembered the part about asking to be held, but when he said it, an embarrassing image filled her brain. How far had she gone in cozying up to this guy that she didn't even know?

Well, as he said, she still had her clothing on. That was good. And Mr. Watson looked like he wished he could sink through the floor and into the center of the earth. That was good, too.

"You found me in my truck—after someone shot at me and I ran off the road?" she asked, struggling to change the subject.

"At you specifically? Is there someone using random motorists for target practice around here?"

It was an interesting question. "I don't know," she said slowly. Then she looked at her watch and puffed out a breath. "But I do know I'd better call the bunkhouse. My hands have to be worried about me."

Glad of the chance to turn away from him, she climbed out from under the covers and sat on the side of the bed, then picked up the phone from the bedside table and dialed.

Jake, one of her ranch hands, answered immediately. "We were worried about you. Are you stuck in town?"

She hesitated for a moment, wavering between truthfulness and the need to make sure her ranch hand wasn't worried. "No. I had some trouble on the road."

"The storm?"

"Um," she answered, thinking that she wasn't going to tell him about the shooting now. Maybe not at all.

"My truck is stuck. But I have a ride. I'll be home soon," she said, then hung up before he could ask any more questions. Half turning, she saw that Watson was looking at her, tension stiffening his face.

"That's one of your men?"

"Yes."

"And you don't want to tell him that someone took a shot at you?"

"I prefer not to worry him."

"Don't you want him on his toes—looking for trouble?"

"I hope there won't be any."

He looked as if he was going to argue about that. Before he could make some kind of point, she said, "I need to go back to town. Right away."

"If someone used you for target practice, you should go to the ranch where you'll be safer."

"What do you mean—if?" she demanded.

"You could be mistaken."

"I'm not. I saw a man up on the bridge with a rifle." She reached into her coat pocket and pulled something out, then flattened her hand, watching his eyes narrow as he saw a rifle slug lying in her palm.

"You thought I dreamed it up, didn't you?"

"Where did you get that?" he asked.

"From the floor of the truck."

"Who do you figure might have wanted to hurt you?"

"I have no idea." She wanted to hear him say he believed her. But that wasn't the important issue at the moment. "I have to get back to town. It's urgent."

Chapter Three

Riley struggled to hold his temper. This woman had fought with him, cuddled with him, argued with him. Now she was telling him she wasn't going to her ranch where she'd be safe. Or relatively safe, given the inconvenient fact that Montana Militia leader Boone Fowler was out there doing Lord knew what.

Since his assignment was to get a job working for her, he stayed where he was and kept his voice low and even. "Do you mind explaining your thinking to me?"

Her expression turned fierce. Standing up, she turned to face him, hands on her hips. "I have to go back to town and see the doctor."

His throat tightened. "Were you hurt when the car went off the road?"

"I don't think so." She stopped and swallowed hard. "But I have to make sure the baby is all right."

He literally felt his jaw drop open, then managed to ask, "What baby?"

He saw color come into her cheeks. "Not that it's any of your business, but I'm pregnant." She kept her gaze steady. "I'm almost seven months along."

"Seven months?" he wheezed. His gaze dropped to her middle, where he detected a small bulge under her man's shirt.

She took in his question and his doubtful look. "I'm carrying small," she said.

"Oh," was the best he could dredge up.

"I have to make sure the baby is okay."

"Yes, right," he answered briskly. He wasn't going to ask her how she'd happened to get pregnant. Instead, he started rushing around the room, collecting outerwear. He had been lying in bed with her, entertaining carnal thoughts, if he were honest about it. And now he found out that she was pregnant.

Damn. He felt like a prize fool. She'd seemed small and fragile in his arms. Well, except for that bulge he hadn't noticed at her middle. And her breasts. They were large. Probably because they were full of milk. No wait, not milk. She wouldn't have milk yet, would she?

He kept his lips pressed together so he wouldn't say anything stupid, and his face turned down because he didn't want her to see the red stain spreading across his cheeks.

She'd been separated from her husband for a year before he'd died. Had she had an affair with one of her cowhands?

When she disappeared into the bathroom, he breathed out a small sigh, then retrieved her gun from the drawer and put it with her coat.

"Jerk," he muttered to himself. He'd been letting himself get turned on by a pregnant woman. That just showed how bad off he was.

Before she could emerge, he pulled on his coat, went out and started furiously clearing the snow from the windshield.

It was less than he'd expected. While he'd been holed up with the little mother, the weather had changed. The storm had abated, leaving the sky a dark blue. And much of the snow on the ground had blown away, the way it could in this part of the state.

Ms. Rogers came out while he was doing the side windows.

"Can I help you?" she asked.

"Almost done," he mumbled, wondering if he'd blown his chances for getting the job. If he had, what the hell was he going to say to the colonel— that he'd screwed up before he ever got to the ranch? On the other hand, his commander hadn't exactly given him sterling information.

The background papers hadn't mentioned that Ms. Rogers was pregnant. What other surprises was he going to encounter?

When he'd cleared off the snow, they climbed into the SUV, and he started back toward town. Since most of the snow was gone, the road was fairly clear.

He split his attention between the driving and his own thoughts. Maybe because he didn't know what the hell he was going to say to Ms. Rogers when they finally discussed the ranch manager situation.

She damn well needed him. But given her previous behavior, he could believe that she might not admit that. And he couldn't tell her that this assignment was of vital importance to the national security of the United States. Big Sky wasn't just on the trail of domestic terrorists. They needed to nail down the connection to King Aleksandr of Lukinburg—then arrest Fowler and his gang.

And he'd better keep reminding himself that no matter how sweet and vulnerable this woman looked, she was sheltering Fowler. And he didn't have a clue about her motives.

He brought himself up short. Vulnerable? Oh, sure.

She would have drilled him if he hadn't gotten

the gun away from her. He stole a glance at her, seeing the set line of her mouth and the tightness of her jaw.

Probably his expression was similar—to avoid giving anything away while he sorted through logic and emotion.

His job was to cozy up to her and get information about her relationship with Fowler. Her pregnancy had suddenly made the assignment more difficult. His own mother had been a single mom, and he knew how hard that would be for Courtney—especially on a horse ranch that was barely making it.

He slid her another look. She had said nothing since they'd started back toward town. Now he felt tension radiating from her.

He turned his head toward her, then followed her gaze. She was staring at the bridge ahead of them—and her vehicle, which was in the field where they'd left it.

Riley slowed, scanning the overpass. "This is where he shot at you?"

She nodded tightly.

While she was feeling off balance, he probed at her with a question. "If the attack was directed at you, who do you think would do it?" he asked.

Her face contorted. "I…don't know."

"Does one of your neighbors have a beef with you?" he probed.

She sighed. "People out here are big on conventional morality. Since I'm pregnant and unmarried, I'm the target of more than a few snide remarks."

"Hmm." He wasn't going to ask her for any clarification. What she did in bed was her own damn business.

He cleared his throat and switched the topic back to attempted murder. "You think the righteous citizens of Spur City would shoot at a pregnant woman?"

"Well, the bullet didn't hit me in the head. Maybe it was just meant to be a warning."

He winced, thinking that if it was a warning shot, the rifleman had been playing fast and loose with her life.

"And the point of a warning would be?"

"Maybe they're trying to get me to move away."

"You mean, as in leave your ranch?"

"I'm not planning to do that!"

She looked beautifully defiant, and he had to remind himself he couldn't trust her. Not until he found out why she'd let Boone Fowler and his gang of thugs onto her ranch.

They had hit the outskirts of the straggly little town that had the audacity to call itself a city. "Drive to the first cross street, then turn right. The clinic is the low building at the end of the block.

Riley knew he was well within the speed limit. When he saw a police car on his tail, he assumed the guy was going somewhere else. But as Riley pulled into the parking lot next to the women's clinic, the cop followed.

He shot Ms. Rogers a quick glance. "You break any laws recently?"

She gave him a startled look. "What are you talking about?"

"There's a cop car pulling in beside us."

She groaned. "Just what I need. Good ol' boy, Sheriff Bobby Pennington."

Riley cut the engine, and she waited a beat before climbing out of the SUV.

Riley hung back, not wanting to step into the middle of anything until he understood the lay of the land.

A big man with a ruddy complexion, mirrored sunglasses and a gray trooper's uniform strode toward her with a purposeful expression on his face. He looked like he owned the street. As he approached, he tipped back his wide-brimmed hat.

She stood with her arms at her sides, and Riley thought she was probably struggling not to fold them protectively across her middle.

"Something I can do for you?" she asked.

"Your truck was found out on the road. Just on the other side of the overpass."

"Yes," she answered, the one syllable coming out clipped, making it clear that she didn't want to continue the discussion.

"What's it doing there?"

"I ran off the road in the snowstorm."

"From what I hear, there's a hole in the front windshield that could have been made by a bullet."

Her face contorted. "News gets around fast."

"Yes it does," he allowed.

"As it happens, the rumors are true. Somebody shot at me."

Riley waited for her to turn over the slug she'd shown him. But she kept it in her pocket.

"You need to come to the office and report the incident."

She hesitated for a moment. "I will. After I stop in at the doctor's office."

"For what? Were you hit?"

She raised her chin. "No, but I want to make sure the baby wasn't hurt in any way, if that's all right with you."

The redness of his complexion deepened. "Yes. Of course. But I want you to file a report before you leave town."

"I will," she promised, and strode into the clinic. Riley hurried to catch up, wondering what had caused the bristly relationship between Ms.

Rogers and the sheriff. Was he hostile to the militia—and hostile to her having them out at the ranch? Was it about her relationship with the town? Or was it something personal?

He tucked the questions into his growing mental file for later investigation.

When he stepped into a room decorated with cute little pictures of babies dressed up like flowers, he wanted to step right back out. But he forced himself to stand there and breathe normally. Ms. Rogers was already at the reception desk, talking to a woman in a white uniform. The rancher glanced back at him. "You might as well sit down."

He nodded, then surveyed the audience looking him up and down as if he was a prize bull at a cattle auction. There were eight women giving him the once-over, ranging in age from teenagers to grandmas. They all sat on molded chairs. The younger ones were all visibly pregnant.

He felt his stomach muscles clench. Trying to keep his expression neutral, he sat down, holding his Western hat in his lap as he focused on a poster beside the desk advertising the opening of a shelter for battered women.

Ms. Rogers broke into his train of thought. "They're going to fit me in, so it shouldn't take too long."

He suppressed the impulse to say thank God.

She hesitated for a moment, then sat in the only empty chair in the room—the one beside him. The seating was tight, and her shoulder brushed his. He knew everyone in the room was watching them, judging the level of intimacy between them.

Two of the women leaned their heads together and began whispering, and he was sure they were discussing him and Ms. Rogers.

To their right, he heard loud voices talking about the new battered-women's shelter. The speakers sounded enthusiastic.

Courtney turned toward them, looking as though she wanted to join in, but she kept her mouth shut.

Luckily she was right about the speedy service. After only ten minutes, a nurse came out and called her name, and she disappeared into the back.

Her departure apparently freed the occupants of the room from restraint.

A gray-haired lady leaned toward him and asked, "So what's your relationship to Mrs. Rogers?"

He blinked, thinking that nine sets of ears—the patients and the receptionist—were tuned in for his answer. And he had five seconds to account for his presence here. "I'm her new ranch manager," he said, hoping that the fib wouldn't matter. If Courtney decided to take him on, then it would be true. If she sent him packing, he'd be the talk of the town. But he wouldn't be around to hear it.

"You know she's not married," the woman said.

"Mmm."

"She was already divorced, but her former husband called her up. They were trying to see if they could get back together. I guess they did that all right. At least for one night."

A teenager in the room giggled.

"He got himself killed in some foreign country after that, leaving her with the ranch and the baby."

"How do you know so much about it?" he asked carefully.

"Everybody knows it. He asked her to meet him for some R&R, and she went rushing off to have a good time with him."

"He was with the CIA or something like that, and he couldn't adjust to the ranch," another woman chipped in. "You look like you're more suited to life out here."

Were they suggesting that he marry Ms. Rogers—to make an honest woman of her?

"She's a handful," someone else murmured, and he wasn't sure exactly who had made the comment. He'd already discovered the truth of that statement.

He slouched down in his seat, hoping that his body language discouraged further conversation.

Courtney returned a few moments later looking vastly relieved.

He saw the peanut gallery eyeing her, then him, then both of them. He stood. "How's the baby?"

"The doctor say's she's fine."

"It's a girl?" he asked.

"Yes."

"Your new ranch manager is a good man," someone said. "You should rely on him."

When Mrs. Rogers's gaze shot to him, Riley wished he could sink through the floor.

She looked as though she wanted to set the speaker straight. Before she could bad-mouth him, he took her arm and steered her through the door.

As soon as they were on the street, she turned fierce eyes to him. "What did Sandra mean—my new ranch manager?"

He struggled to keep his voice even and reasonable. "As soon as you left, one of those busybodies asked me what I was to you. What did you want me to say—that I was your lover? Or maybe I picked you up along the road, and we got friendly real fast."

She had opened her mouth to make another comment. But she shut it again. He watched her struggling to get control of her temper before saying, "You don't have the job yet."

"I'm aware of that."

"We need to finish our job interview," she murmured, stepping into a small courtyard where the walls of two buildings cut the wind.

He followed her into the small enclosure. "Okay."

She gave him a narrow-eyed look. "You said you grew up on a ranch and that you've worked on several spreads in Texas and Wyoming."

"Yes."

"And you did a stint in the Special Forces."

"Yes."

"My husband was in the service, and he hated ranch life," she said with a challenge in her voice.

"Well, I'm not him. I came home to ranch work after the service," he said, the lie sticking in his throat.

But it seemed to satisfy her...for the time being. He could also tell she hadn't quite made up her mind.

She sighed. "I'd better go to the sheriff's office."

"I'll go with you."

"Why?"

"Is that a trick question? I think he's the kind of guy who will behave better if there's a witness along—particularly a witness of the male variety."

"You have him pegged there."

"You've known him a long time?"

"No. He's new in town."

That was interesting, Riley thought. "What brought him here?"

"Maybe he likes being a big fish in a little pond."

"He likes to throw his weight around?"

"Unfortunately, yes. And since he got here, the town has become a lot more…lawless."

"Like how?"

"Like an increase in cattle rustling."

"And shooting incidents out on the highway?"

"Yes," she muttered.

They walked across the street to the office. Courtney breathed out a little sigh when the clerk told her that Pennington was on his dinner break. Instead of enduring an interview, she was able to fill out a form reporting the gunshot incident, and they were out of the office in under twenty minutes.

"You're not going to leave the slug with him?" Riley asked.

"No."

"Why not?"

"Because it's evidence, and I don't want it to disappear."

Riley considered that as they climbed back into the SUV.

COURTNEY WANTED to get out of town as quickly as possible—and back to the ranch. But she couldn't leave yet.

"Mike's Gas Station is at the edge of town. We need to stop there and arrange to have my truck towed."

"Yeah, I saw it."

On the way to Mike's, she called Jake Bradley again and told him she'd stopped at the doctor's to make sure the baby was okay. Jake had been at the ranch since her grade-school years. She knew he'd be concerned.

As she arranged to have the truck towed and fixed, she watched Mike eyeing her and Riley Watson with interest. But she wasn't going to offer explanations.

Finally they started home. And it was a relief to be away from people who wanted to ask questions about her relationship with this good-looking stranger. She could just imagine some of the speculation. Had she hired him because he was young and handsome? Did she hope he'd marry her and take over the ranch? Was she looking for a guy to warm her bed at night?

She cringed inwardly. He might be attractive and sexy and strong and reliable, but that didn't mean she was going to climb into bed with him—again.

That "again" made her cheeks hot, even though bedding down with him had been perfectly innocent. She hoped.

She also hoped that Harold Avery, the old geezer who owned the motel hadn't seen her. If he had, the news would be all over town. She wanted to ask what Watson had said when he'd checked in, but she kept her lips pressed together.

Damn. The knowledge that she and this man were already the subject of speculation made her want to tell him she'd changed her mind about the job. Yet she silently admitted that she'd be acting against her best interests. And she knew darn well that she wasn't being fair to him.

It was after dark when they approached the bridge again, and she couldn't help the little frisson of fear that slithered down her spine.

When he slowed, her gaze shot to him. "What are you doing?"

"Going up there to have a look."

"No." Courtney heard herself say, the one syllable coming out high and strained.

"Now that we're not in a hurry to get to the doctor's, I want to find out what happened."

"The guy's long gone. And you'll just be poking around in the dark."

"Maybe he left a shell casing to go along with that bullet. Maybe he dropped a cigarette butt. Or leftovers from his lunch." Without asking permission, Watson pulled to the side of the road.

She knitted her gloved hands together, holding tight, fighting her fears. She felt exposed out here on the highway, but she knew Watson was right. If there was still some evidence up on the bridge, they ought to find out what it was before it conveniently disappeared. Not that she was accusing the sheriff of anything dishonest. But there had been too many cases around here lately where the bad guys got away.

Watson opened the glove compartment and pulled out a flashlight. Then he stepped out into the cold and closed the door quickly to keep the heat inside.

She forced herself to sit quietly while the man who might or might not be her new ranch hand scaled the bridge abutment.

The clouds had blown away, and the moon had come out. In its pale light, she saw him move with agility and grace. Under other circumstances, she might have enjoyed watching him climb.

He made it to the road, then strode onto the bridge, where he switched on the light and shone it down toward the blacktop.

When he disappeared from view below the concrete railing, she felt her breath catch. But she could still see the light moving around up there.

The man was out of sight for several minutes during which she sat in the SUV gripping the edge of the seat.

She had just decided to go look for him when he popped back into view.

From his position above the highway, he waved to her, then began to climb down

"What did you find?" she demanded when he'd slipped behind the wheel and started the engine.

"He was a careful bastard. There might have been footprints in the snow, but he scuffed them away so I can't tell the size of his boot."

"Any shell casings?"

"No. He took them with him. And if he drank any coffee or smoked any cigarettes, he took the leavings away, too. Like I said, he was careful— or well trained. He could be a guy with a military background," he said, dropping the observation into the conversation, then watching her closely.

She wasn't sure what response he expected, but she only shrugged.

Watson drove to the other side of the bridge, then stopped beside her truck.

"We should unload your supplies, before some of them disappear," he said.

She wanted to tell him that people around here didn't steal from each other, but she wasn't sure if that was true anymore.

"Yes. Let me help you."

He cleared his throat. "You shouldn't be lifting stuff, should you?"

"Nothing heavy. But there are things I can manage."

"Okay." He pulled off the road in back of the truck and cut the engine, but he didn't immediately open the door.

She sensed his tension, and she wondered suddenly if he had some additional information about the man who had been up on the bridge. In response, she felt her chest tighten.

When he spoke, his voice had turned gruff, and it took several seconds for his question to filter into her consciousness, because it was the last thing she had been expecting.

"So…have you made up your mind about hiring me?" he asked.

Chapter Four

Riley waited for Courtney's answer with his breath frozen in his lungs. In the hours since he'd met her, this assignment had become more than a job. Maybe because the flesh-and-blood woman was so much more complicated—so much more appealing—than the woman he'd read about in a briefing folder. She didn't even look much like her pictures, which was why he hadn't recognized her.

He wanted to ask her about Boone Fowler—about why she'd let a lowlife jerk like him onto her property. But he knew that was precisely the wrong approach. And it was against orders, too. Because as far as she was concerned, he didn't know a damn thing about the militia leader. So all he could do was sit there waiting for her to decide his immediate future.

He had the feeling she was still weighing the pros and cons of her decision.

Instead of answering, she asked a question—something more specific than she'd put to him in town. "What's the best material for a corral fence?"

So she was giving him a test. He was glad he had the background to say, "It depends on what you're after. Looks, utility or price. Split rail is the cheapest. Those who go in for show favor white painted boards. Outside the main paddock, I like wire, with one line of electricity. To keep the stock from leaning on the fence."

She nodded, then asked, "How do you tie a foal when you're first training him?"

"The first few times, you want to make sure he's not tied hard and fast. He might pull and injure his neck. I'd introduce a truck or car inner tube between him and the fence. That will act like a fat rubber band and offer some give."

"What's a chestnut?"

"I take it you don't mean something roasting on an open fire? We're talking about a horny, insensitive growth on a horse's legs."

"How would you treat it?"

"Trim it short and neat."

"I guess you know horses."

"Yeah."

She heaved in a breath and let it out. "You have the job."

"Thank you," he said simply as they stood together on the frozen ground.

"You'll sleep in the bunkhouse with the other hands," she added, as though she felt it necessary to make it very clear that their afternoon in bed had been an aberration.

"I understand," he answered, as he undid the hooks that held the tarp covering the supplies in the back of the pickup.

"It's comfortable, but it's nothing fancy."

"I sure don't need fancy. Just a bed and a chest of drawers will do," he answered.

"And I assume the salary we discussed is satisfactory."

"Yes, ma'am." He turned his attention to the supplies. "Does it look like everything's there?"

She carefully inspected her purchases. "Yes."

"Good." He opened the back of the SUV and began loading sacks of feed.

By the time they had finished, the back of his SUV was crammed to the roof, and the temperature had dropped sharply.

"Tell me about the Golden Saddle," he said as he turned on the headlights and started down the highway again.

"Well, you already know we have twenty mares and five stallions. Most are quarter horses. But we have some Thoroughbred bloodlines, too. That might be our problem. Our prices are high, and the demand for horses like ours is falling." She cleared her throat. "We could sell more to working cattle ranches. But that would mean we'd have to train them with cattle. And I don't have the staff to raise both horses and cattle at the moment."

"You didn't mention any 'problem' when you advertised for a manager," he said carefully, although he already knew that she was barely turning a profit.

"Well, that's not the kind of thing I'd advertise, would I?" she snapped.

"Do you have any other source of income—besides the sale of horses?" he asked.

"I rent some unused buildings," she answered.

"To whom?"

She hesitated a moment before answering, "A, um, group of…survivalists."

"Oh, yeah?" She must be referring to Boone Fowler's militia. So were they styling themselves as survivalists? Or was that her term for them—because she thought it was more politically correct?

She was staring hard at him. "You object to my renting to them?" she asked sharply.

He knew he'd better be careful about stepping over the line with his answer. She owned the ranch. He was her hired help.

Even so, he had to fight the impulse to tell her about his experiences in Boone Fowler's prison camp. Instead he kept his voice even as he said, "It's not my place to object. Not if they mind their own business."

He wanted to ask how they happened to pick the Golden Saddle Ranch. And where—exactly—they were located on her property. But he didn't want to seem too interested, so he held back the questions.

"The entrance to the ranch is right up ahead," she said.

He slowed down, then turned in at a horseshoe-shaped archway.

They bumped up a gravel road that was pocked with potholes.

Floodlights illuminated the ranch yard, and he saw a low stone-and-timber house with a wide front porch, which he knew had been built early in the previous century. The structure looked solid, but in the floodlights he could see that the trim around the window frames needed painting. Probably she'd do that when she got some spare cash.

The bunkhouse and barn were nearby. And another building that he assumed was used for storage.

He pulled up in front of the house. "We should unload what you need to take inside."

"And you can put the SUV in the storage building for the night—then unload the rest in the morning."

"Fine."

Apparently, some of Ms. Rogers's hands had been listening for her to arrive, because two of them came striding toward the SUV.

One was a short, grizzled guy with the bow legged gait of a man who has spent much of his life in the saddle. He appeared to be in his fifties. The other was taller than his companion and younger than Riley. Both men wore jeans, heavy winter coats and Western hats.

Riley and Ms. Rogers climbed out of the vehicle. The two men eyed him with undisguised interest. But it was different from the appraisal of the people in town. These guys seemed to be protective of Ms. Rogers—although that could be an act, of course.

"Jake Bradley, Kelly Manning, this is Riley Watson," she said. "I told you I was considering him for ranch manager, and he's going to take the job."

"Good to meet you." He shook hands with both of them. They helped Courtney unload her groceries. Then he drove to the storage shed and left his vehicle inside. Finally he strode to the bunkhouse.

Up close, he could see it was a little newer than the main house, but also rustic. And it was set up like a private residence, with a living room, dining room, kitchen and several bedrooms in the back. All the furniture looked comfortable but well-worn.

The man named Kelly showed him to a bedroom. "There are three bathrooms," he said, opening several doors along the hall.

"How many hands do you have?"

"Just three at the moment. Me and Jake and Billy. They'll be along later."

So the ranch was understaffed. He'd have to inspect the property in the morning. There was no point in stumbling around in the dark.

Setting down his duffel bag, he longed to close the bedroom door and lie down.

Instead he squared his shoulders and followed Kelly back to the kitchen.

Jake had just taken the lid off a big pot of chili…and Riley's stomach growled.

"That smells good."

Jake made a grunting sound.

"So you like working for Ms. Rogers?" he asked.

"Yup," Jake answered. Apparently he was a man of few words.

Riley scuffed his foot against a worn floorboard. "She seemed kind of hyper."

Jake's head snapped toward him. "She's got a

shrinking income. She's got herself a kid to raise on her own—with the whole town acting like she did something wrong. And—"

He stopped short.

Riley wanted to ask, "And what?" But he kept his mouth shut. He should have gotten the lay of the land before coming out with any kind of strong observation. Holding up his hands, he said, "Whoa. I didn't mean any disrespect."

"You blame her for being hyper?" Jake pressed.

"I admire her—for truckin' on. But it was a shock to find out she was pregnant."

"Her husband was in the Special Forces. And he bought the farm on assignment in Lukinburg."

Riley mumbled something appropriate, then changed the subject to the ranch acreage. They discussed the spread for a few minutes, then Jake said, "You want some dinner?"

"I'd appreciate it. Your chili sure does smell good."

Kelly and Jake both joined him at the table. Billy Cramer came in during the meal, and Jake made the introductions.

Riley knew the other men were sizing him up, just like he was doing with them. Could one of them have been the man who had shot at Courtney from the bridge?

He didn't know, but he was going to find out.

RILEY WOKE WHEN HE HEARD the hands moving around the bunkhouse. When he arrived in the kitchen twenty minutes later, the rest of them were already at the table, eating eggs, bacon and toast.

The ranch might be in financial trouble, but Courtney Rogers was feeding her men well.

A television in the corner was tuned to the weather channel. It seemed they were in for another cold, blustery day. Par for the course in Montana in winter. But at least snow wasn't in the forecast. Of course, he'd checked the weather yesterday. And there had been no mention of snow then, either.

After eating some of the food and complimenting the chef, he turned to Kelly and said, "So, could you show me around the spread?"

The young man looked startled. "Me? Jake's been here a lot longer."

Jake shifted in his chair. "Go ahead. I'll clean up here."

Kelly nodded.

Riley dressed warmly, grabbed some carrots from the refrigerator, then followed Kelly to the barn, the most modern structure he'd seen so far on the ranch.

Unless one of the men had gotten up early and scurried over here to make sure the work area looked good for the new ranch manager, everything seemed to be up to snuff. The stalls were clean. The well-groomed horses had plenty of food and water. And the equipment in the tack room was in good condition and neatly stored.

He stopped to greet the horses in the stalls, calling them by the names on the small plates at each door and offering carrots, which were readily accepted.

They paused by a stall with a filly named Irma. A protective boot was wrapped around her left foreleg.

"What happened to her?" Riley asked.

"She overreached and bruised herself—the way they do sometimes."

Kicked her front leg with her back, Riley mentally translated. "Yeah, that can be a problem. How are you treating the injury?"

"We started with cold hosing three times a day. Now we're on to warm, dry bandages."

He fed Irma a carrot, which she gobbled up, telling him her appetite was good. On a more prosperous ranch the owner might have called out the vet. But he knew it wasn't unusual for owners to treat minor problems, which certainly saved money.

Another filly named Buttercup was obviously very pregnant.

"When is she due?" Riley asked.

"In a few weeks."

They discussed some of the other horses, then Riley continued on his fact-finding mission. "Who's been running things?"

"Jake."

"He's doing a good job." He hesitated for a moment. "So, would he resent someone taking over?"

Kelly scuffed his foot against the hard-packed dirt. "I guess you'll have to ask him."

Yeah, sure.

"Has there been any vandalism at the ranch?"

Kelly looked uncomfortable.

"What?" Riley pressed.

"We got some renters. They're using the back forty for a garbage dump."

"What renters?"

"Ask the boss lady."

"Okay," Riley answered, then cleared his throat. "I noticed she took some flack in town. Do the men on the ranch—" he stopped and fumbled for what to say "—support her."

"Everybody here now is on her side."

"Now?" Riley probed.

"There was a guy here—Greg Nichols. He made some...nasty comments."

"To her face?"

"Not likely. But they got back to her, and she asked him to lcavc."

"Would Nichols make trouble for her?" Riley was thinking of the man who had shot at her from the bridge. If he knew her routine, he could have lain in wait for her. Or someone out here could have called him.

"Maybe."

"What does he look like?"

"Blond hair. Blue eyes. A big scar on his right cheek."

So he'd be easy to spot, Riley mused.

They finished the tour back at the barn. Riley could go to the house and start perusing the books. But he didn't want to barge in on Ms. Rogers. Their first meeting had been pretty crazy. Maybe he should give her some space. And himself, too. Taking the coward's route, he decided to have a look around some of the ranch acreage. He found himself wondering if he'd find any signs of the guy named Greg Nichols. What if he were hiding out on the ranch? Was he watching Courtney's activities?

With a silent curse he reminded himself he wasn't supposed to be looking for Nichols. He was supposed to locate Boone Fowler's militia group so he could report back to Big Sky.

Of course, Nichols could be with Fowler. So maybe if he found the militia group, he'd kill two birds with one stone.

AFTER SADDLING UP a stallion named Monty, he rode east across a shallow river into rugged country with rolling hills covered by dry grass. Rugged snowcapped mountains rose in the background like sentinels.

But he could easily skirt the patches of snow that still lay in the valley shadows.

Of course, the ranch encompassed almost ten thousand acres, so there was a lot of territory to cover. But Big Sky had done aerial surveillance and pinpointed some areas to investigate.

He brought Monty to a halt and turned in the saddle, taking in the wide-open spaces that stretched around him. Out here, he and the horse might have been the only two living creatures in the world.

After two hours on the range, he found nothing out of the ordinary. So he headed back, then spent the rest of the day asking more questions, unobtrusively watching the men do their jobs and giving the horses a more thorough inspection. And all the time he was aware of Ms. Rogers's absence.

That evening he joined the rest of the hands at dinner, working hard to convey the impression that he was a regular guy who just wanted to fit in to the established patterns of the Golden Saddle Ranch.

But when he went to sleep, he had no control

over his unconscious mind. He dreamed about Courtney. Dreamed about holding her in his arms in a bed the way he had in that motel room. Only, in his sleep, the encounter hadn't been quite so innocent. He'd started taking her clothes off, like a man uncovering buried treasure. And her hands had moved just as eagerly over him.

He woke up angry with himself. In practical terms he was thinking that probably he should have gone out and gotten laid before he took this job. Then he wouldn't be so focused on Courtney Rogers. She fascinated him. Exasperated him. Attracted him. She'd been ready to defend herself when she thought he was the guy who'd taken a shot at her. But she was hiding out from her own ranch manager.

COURTNEY STEPPED BACK from the window. She'd been watching for Riley Watson, and he'd just stridden across the ranch yard and into the barn.

He had an unsettling effect on her, like no one she'd ever met. He was so damn self-contained, yet below the surface she could sense his mind working.

Too bad he was the sexiest man she'd met in a long time. That was another major problem. He had made her feel hot and needy, just from the way he looked at her.

And she knew that he found her attractive. That was part of the lure of the man for her—the exhilaration of knowing that he was responding to her, even in her condition.

Her lips firmed. She should be focused on the baby, not some cowboy who had just stepped into her life. Or was she so eager for attention, that she glommed on to the first guy who came along?

She stalked down the hall, then stopped short at the room that she was fixing up as a nursery. For Emily. Or maybe Hannah. She wasn't sure of the name yet, and she hated not being able to discuss her choices with anyone.

She stroked her hand over her abdomen. "What do you think, Emily? Do you like that name? Or is Hannah better?"

She'd let her imagination blossom as she'd decorated the room. The walls were a light green, with a colorful garden of flowers and a picket fence running around the bottom three feet of the walls. And in a fit of whimsy, she'd painted the ceiling blue and added fluffy white clouds.

She fingered a pink and white blanket she'd bought on sale from an online company. Too bad nobody in Spur City had thought to give her a baby shower. With money so tight, she could have used the gifts. And she would have loved someone making a fuss over her.

That last thought made her grimace. It sounded as if she was feeling sorry for herself. And that wasn't true. She was going to make the best life she could for herself and her daughter.

And she wasn't going to let Riley Watson think she was a coward. Because she wasn't. She simply hadn't been prepared to meet anyone like him—not now.

Marching out of the baby's room, she hurried to the front hall and pulled on her coat. It was about time she stopped hiding in her own house. But just as she stepped out the door, she saw the man ride past who had been in her thoughts—and he didn't look as if he was just taking Monty around the ranch yard.

RILEY RODE NORTH into an area where the landscape was flatter. A couple of miles from the ranch yard, he caught sight of something interesting through the trees and ordered Monty to a halt. Just visible through a screen of branches, he could see an old cabin.

He'd better check the place out.

The militia could be using it—or that Gary Nichols guy could be squatting here.

He dismounted and tied the horse to a low pine branch. Then crept slowly forward, moving from tree to tree in case somebody took a notion to shoot at him.

The cabin sat in a large clearing. He observed it from cover for several minutes, then stepped into the open. Now that he was exposed to view, he moved more rapidly.

Maybe he should have been paying better attention to where he put his feet.

The ground was scattered with brush. When he crossed a patch with a heavy accumulation of branches and leaves, the surface gave way under his feet with a ripping sound. Before he could catch himself, he was tumbling into blackness… and cursing his own stupidity.

Chapter Five

Riley dropped through space, struggling to stay on his feet. Knees bent, he landed with a thud. As far as he could tell, he was at the bottom of a pit someone had deliberately dug.

Daylight poured in from the hole where he'd broken through. And as he tried to move his feet, he found they were stuck between some wickedly pointed stakes poking out of the ground.

They were lethal enough to pierce flesh, and he was damn lucky that he hadn't landed on his ass.

He took a quick physical inventory, moving his arms and legs, then twisting his torso. It appeared that he hadn't seriously injured himself in the fall, which was also damn lucky.

He looked up, inspecting the ragged hole in the brush through which he'd fallen. So—was this an animal trap… Or was this a man trap?

He brought his attention back to the broken roof above him. It looked like slender sticks had been placed across the pit. They provided just enough support to hold the brush in place. And he'd stepped through the surface—like a damn fool out for a stroll in the park.

Well, that mistake was in the past. Now he'd better figure out how to get out before whoever had set the trap came back to see if he'd caught anything.

The walls of the hole were too far apart for him to brace his back and feet and climb up that way. He decided to try to pull out the stakes, work them into the side and make a ladder. He had almost freed one, when a noise from above made him tense.

Footsteps.

Someone was up there, crunching across the open space. Coming to scoop him up.

Well, he wasn't going to stand here waiting for the trapper to get the drop on him. Pulling his gun from the holster at his waist, he held it pointed upward in a two-handed grip, ready to shoot anybody who attacked him.

When a shadow fell across the opening, his finger tensed on the trigger.

Then somebody called his name. "Riley?"

A curse sprang to his lips. He knew that voice. It was Courtney Rogers, and he felt his heart stop and start again in double time. He had come within a hair's breadth of shooting her.

"Riley, answer me. Are you all right?" she shouted down at him, the question shaking with anxiety.

Her face appeared over the side of the opening above him. When she saw him standing so far below her, she gasped. "Are you all right?" she asked again.

"Yeah," he answered, then followed with a question of his own. "What the hell are you doing here—if you don't mind my asking?"

"I wanted to talk to you."

"You had all of yesterday and a couple hours this morning to do that."

He saw her face contort. "I was working my way up to it."

"Oh, yeah? What does that mean?"

"I think you can figure it out."

He wanted clarification. But he didn't think he would get it now. They were both silent for several seconds while he mulled over her confession.

"How did you find me here?" he demanded.

"I saw you saddle up and ride out. So I decided to follow you."

"You're alone?" he asked, hearing the strained sound of his own voice.

"Yes."

He was aghast to hear the next words that

popped out of his mouth. "Why are you still riding? I mean…in your condition?"

"My doctor says I can ride—until it feels uncomfortable."

"Okay," he muttered, because decisions about her pregnancy were none of his business. Besides, he had more immediate problems to deal with, like not getting them both killed by whoever had dug this hole.

Fear for her leaped inside him, but he made his voice crisp. "So let's figure out how to get me out."

"Yes."

"I don't suppose you have a rope?"

She made a clucking sound. "I used to carry one. I figured I wouldn't be roping horses anytime soon."

"Well, we need an alternate plan. I was going to use the stakes down here for a ladder, but that eats up time. Are there any poles up there? Something I could use to haul myself up."

"Let me look."

She was gone for a long time, and his hands clenched and unclenched as he waited for her to reappear. He wanted to call out to her, but he knew that would give away too much—if someone else was hanging around up there.

After what seemed like eons, he heard footsteps coming back, and he moved to the side of the pit and held his gun down beside his leg.

"Courtney?"

"Yes. Watch out. I'm sending a branch down."

The sky above him was suddenly obscured by a large mass of green. It slipped into the hole and landed, quivering, at the bottom.

"Can you use that?" Courtney called.

"Clever idea. I just hope I'm not too heavy."

The pine branch was large and sturdy, as big around as a small tree.

"How did you get this thing loose?" he called up to the woman who looked anxiously over the edge of the pit.

"There's a knife in my saddle bag. I used it to make a cut. Then I pulled down on it until it broke."

He was tempted to yell at her that she shouldn't have been doing anything so strenuous. But he had no idea of her physical limitations. And right now, his main job was to get the hell out of here.

He set the limb upright, cut end down, and leaned it against the side of the pit. After making sure it was secure, he tested the branches that came off the sides. They were slender and bent easily, and he hoped they'd hold his weight. Maybe if he distributed it well, he'd be okay.

And at any rate, he had no real choice. Without a rope or a ladder, the pine branch was his best chance of escape.

Courtney leaned over the opening, looking down at him.

"Stand back. When I come up, it's going to be fast."

She did as he asked while he studied the pattern of the side limbs. Then he reached up and grabbed an upper branch at the same time that he found a foothold near the ground.

Feeling like a monkey on steroids, he began to climb, praying that he made it to the top before the ladder fell apart.

Needles whipped him in the face as he climbed upward. He ignored them and kept going. He was halfway up when the support under his left foot gave way with a loud crack. Above him he heard Courtney gasp.

He wanted to tell her he was okay, but he couldn't spare the breath. All he could do was keep scrambling upward.

He was almost to the top, where the limbs were more slender. One of them gave way. Then another. As he started to drop backward, Courtney's arm shot out. Her fingers grabbed the collar of his jacket, stopping his downward plunge just enough that he could grab the lip of the hole and haul himself over the edge.

He flopped onto the ground, breathing hard from the exertion. Damn! He should have added more sessions in the gym to the list of preparations he'd made before coming here.

Courtney came down beside him, her hand gripping his arm. "Riley, are you all right?" she gasped. "Riley, answer me!"

He rolled onto his back, staring up at her. And the look of profound relief in her eyes, coupled with his own roiling emotions was too much for him.

Without giving himself time to think, he reached for her, pulling her to him.

She could have resisted, but she came willingly into his arms, sprawling on top of him.

He was conscious of the cold, sharp air around him, the blue of the sky above him, the knowledge that he was alive and safe—thanks to the woman who was now in his embrace. Maybe he needed to express his gratitude. Maybe he needed to clarify what he was feeling at this moment.

Inch by inch, giving her the opportunity to untangle herself, he pulled her mouth down to his own trembling lips. To his relief and astonishment, she came willingly. Maybe she meant the gesture as a quick kiss—a way to tell him how glad she was he had made it out of the trap. But once her lips connected with his, everything changed.

He felt the world spinning around him, felt something hot and rich leap between himself and the woman in his arms.

He couldn't speak for her motives. And he didn't even know if he could trust her. But his brush with death had made him reckless.

His hand stroked into her thick hair, holding her where he wanted her as he angled his head so that he could deepen the kiss.

One taste of her, and the only thought in his mind was kissing her with all the passion suddenly welling inside him.

And he was positive the reaction wasn't one-sided.

The kiss grew frantic as her mouth moved against his and her hands stroked over his shoulders. Pushing his hat off, she winnowed her fingers through his hair.

He knew she'd been working to keep her distance from him since they'd climbed out of bed two days ago. Suddenly everything had changed. She was kissing him with all the sensuality he'd conjured up in his dream. And his response was no less fiery.

He held her tight against his body, rocking her in his arms, urgency making his hands tremble.

He wanted more. But not here. Not on the cold ground. He wanted her in a nice warm bed, like the one in the motel room.

Yet he hadn't abandoned sanity entirely, and he understood in some corner of his mind that what they were doing was wrong.

Then one of the horses whinnied, reminding him exactly where they were.

Her head jerked up, and she glanced wildly around, looking as confused as he felt.

He growled out an apology. "Lord, Courtney, I'm sorry."

She rolled away from him, staring up at the sky, breathing hard. "I…I'm sorry. I shouldn't have—"

"Don't blame yourself. It was all my fault," he said quickly, even when he knew that wasn't precisely the truth. To his surprise he found his need to protect her was stronger than his need to act like the innocent party here.

He sat up, snatching his hat off the ground and setting it on his head again, using the brim to shade his face.

"You were glad to get out of that trap," she said in a soft voice.

"God, yes," he answered, grateful that she'd given him some kind of plausible excuse for the inexcusable.

He wanted to look away. No, he wanted to scramble up and run for the hills. But his own discomfort was a secondary consideration. Now that they were face-to-face, and he could see her properly, he asked one of the questions he hadn't bothered with earlier. "Who dug that pit?"

She took her lower lip between her teeth. "I have no idea."

She looked genuinely perplexed and upset. Still, he pushed for answers. "It's on your property."

"Yes—but I haven't been out this way in months. Except for trips into town, I've stayed close to the house since…"

"Since what?" he demanded. "Since the baby? Or have there been problems out here that you haven't shared with me?"

She looked away.

Moments ago he'd vowed to keep his hands off her. Now he reached out and took her by the chin, bringing her face back so that she had to meet his gaze. "I think you'd better tell me what the hell has been happening on the ranch. And don't tell me 'nothing.' I can see in your face that it's not 'nothing.'"

"I don't owe you any explanations."

"Yes you do—if you don't want me to pack up and get the hell out of here."

"Maybe you should," she said in a small voice.

The flat way she said it made his insides knot, and he heard desperate words tumbling out of his mouth. "I thought you were a smart lady. What are you going to do, send me away because you're afraid to level with me?"

He watched a war going on inside her. "No," she finally said.

"No...what?"

"I'm not going to cut off my nose to spite my face."

"Then tell me what the ranch manager at the Golden Saddle has to deal with—besides the normal business of running the spread."

She sighed. "Some things have happened. I mean, like some fences down. A...a dead skunk at my back door."

He swore. "Has anyone shot at you before yesterday? And don't lie to me."

"No!"

"Who do you think is responsible for the problems?"

"People from town."

"Who specifically?"

She shrugged.

He sighed. He wanted to keep at her. He had a feeling she could give him some leads if she wanted to. But she had pressed her lips together.

"Why don't you want to answer the question?"

"I don't want to make things worse for myself in Spur City."

He'd love to refute that logic. But they had more immediate issues to deal with. Turning, he gestured toward the old cabin. "What's this place used for?" he asked.

"Nothing."

"Then what's it doing here?"

"Years ago my dad used to run some cattle. Ranch hands would come out here if they needed to stay with the herd. But nobody's been here recently."

"Not that you know of." He raised his head toward the darkened windows. "I'm going to have a look."

He saw fear leap in her eyes. "What are you worried about—that I'll find out you're lying?"

"No!"

He sighed, "Okay, you stay here. I'll go inside."

"What do you expect to find?"

"A smuggling operation? Drugs from Canada?" She snorted.

Without inviting further conversation, he picked himself up, brushed off his clothing with as much dignity as he could muster and turned toward the cabin. If anyone was inside—like a militia man or ex-employee Greg Nichols—he hadn't shown up to investigate the scene out here, which included the owner of the Golden Saddle and her new ranch manager rolling around in the dirt. Or whatever the hell they'd been doing.

Riley walked toward the cabin, focused on external threats, partly because he didn't want to think about his personal relationship with Courtney Rogers.

Taking no chances, he crouched over, making himself as small a target as possible as he crossed the twenty-five yards that separated him from the weathered building.

As he moved cautiously forward, he divided his attention between the cabin and the ground under his feet, looking for additional booby traps.

Which was why he saw the innocent-looking wire lying on a patch of pine needles a split second after his foot had crossed it. Well-honed training snapped into place.

Without even thinking about what he was doing, he threw himself onto hard-packed dirt.

Chapter Six

Riley's hat flew off as he went down. He covered his head with his arms, just as the cabin exploded in a massive blast that seemed to shake the mountains.

Wood, stone and metal rained down around him. He winced when something heavy landed on his butt. Twisting onto his side, he shook the debris off, then grimaced as an ax fell, blade down, a few inches from his shoulder.

His heart leaped into his throat as his thoughts turned to Courtney. Lord, had she followed his directions? Was she safe? He had to find out. Yet he knew it wasn't safe to move yet. It felt like hours, although it had to be less than a minute before the deadly shower stopped.

Cautiously he lifted his head, then heard a high, anxious voice calling his name.

Courtney. She sounded scared—or hurt.

Rolling onto his side, he saw her picking her way toward him. He went rigid.

"Stay back!" he shouted, but she kept coming across the littered field…where all kinds of dangers might lurk.

"Stay back!" he ordered again. Clambering to his feet, he hurried toward her, cursing when his boot came down on a piece of twisted metal.

He stopped a few feet from her, and she looked as if she wanted to reach for him again. But he knew what had happened last time they'd touched. They'd ended up plastered together on the ground. So he clenched his hands into fists at his side and kept his distance.

Her gaze swept frantically over him. "Riley, are you all right?" she gasped out.

"I think so." Taking inventory, he flexed his arms and legs. He'd have a few bruises. But everything seemed to be in working order.

While she was inspecting him, he was doing the same to her, his gaze inevitably descending to her middle, and he was amazed all over again how little her pregnancy showed under her man's shearling coat.

She seemed to be all right. But he had to ask, "What about you—did you stay out of range?"

"Yes," she answered, still sounding stunned.

While she was busy grappling with the aftermath of the explosion, he pressed his advantage again, "What happened?"

Her eyes grew big. "The...the cabin...exploded," she stuttered.

"Yeah, that's obvious," he answered dryly. "The question is...why?"

"I...don't know."

He had to take her word for that. She wouldn't have let him walk toward another deadly ambush. Would she? No. Not after that kiss. He hoped!

"So do you think the same guy who shot at you left a couple of booby traps? I mean the pit and the trip wire?"

She shook her head helplessly. "I told you, I haven't come out this way much in the past few months. Creating dangers out here would be an inefficient way to go after me."

"Yeah." He would have liked to bombard her with questions about the militia. But she hadn't been very forthcoming about her "survivalist" tenants.

What was going on out here exactly. Were the cabin and the pit part of a training exercise. That was pretty rough training. But he already knew that Boone Fowler played rough.

He turned and glanced at the rubble strewn over the ground. It might yield some clues. But looking for them was probably a dangerous plan, given the way things were going around the Golden Saddle.

"I think we've had enough excitement for one morning," he said. "Maybe we should get back to the ranch yard. If the sheriff were anyone besides Bobby Pennington, I'd report this. Under the circumstances, we might as well not bother."

Relief flooded her face. "Yes."

He made direct eye contact with her. "But perhaps you'd better stay close to the house until we find out what's going on around here."

"I can't stay locked inside," she objected.

Like you did yesterday and this morning when you were avoiding me? Again he kept the observation to himself.

"Stick around the ranch yard. And if you're planning to go farther, check in with me."

When she seemed to be getting ready to object, he played his ace in the hole. "If you don't want to do it for yourself, do it for the baby."

She sucked in a sharp breath. "That's not playing fair."

"I'm trying to keep you safe."

"You hardly know me."

Before he could stop himself, he said, "But neither one of us is going to pretend that I don't care, are we?"

He saw her swallow, then nodded. She looked as if she was going to ask him a question, but she kept silent.

"What?"

"Nothing. We should get back."

So what issue was she ducking now?

She turned and hurried toward the stand of trees, and he caught up with her, his hand closing over her shoulder.

"Let me go first."

"You don't think something else could happen, do you?"

"At this point, I'm not taking any chances."

She hesitated for a moment, and he held his breath, worried that she was going to demonstrate her stubborn, inconvenient, independent streak.

Apparently, common sense overcame pride, and she dropped back, allowing him to walk in front of her, scanning the woods as he went.

When a dry branch cracked, he stopped short and drew his gun. Then a small animal scurried away, and he breathed out a sigh.

Looking back at Courtney, he saw the tension on her face, but he didn't bother to comment.

She'd tied her own horse, a palomino named Caramel, near where he'd left Monty.

They rode back to the ranch compound in silence.

As soon as they reached the barn, Kelly rushed up. "What happened out there?"

"One of the old line cabins exploded," Riley answered, watching the younger man's face.

He looked shocked.

Either he didn't have anything to do with it. Or he was a damn good actor.

"I'm going inside. Would you mind taking care of Caramel?" Courtney said.

"Certainly," the ranch hand answered.

Riley breathed out a little sigh, glad that she was following his advice for the moment. Despite his concerns, he couldn't babysit her now. He needed to call Big Sky on his special cell phone and tell them about the new development—and that required privacy.

But when he walked off toward the bunkhouse where he might have some privacy, he saw that Jake had spotted him and was following. He changed course and pretended to be making a close inspection of the corral fences. Jake gave him a long look, then went back to the barn.

After spending some time "inspecting the fence," Riley headed for a stand of trees not far from the ranch yard. Ducking behind one, he pulled out the special cell phone and made the call.

Joseph Brown answered.

"Riley, we've been waiting for you to check in. How's the assignment going?"

"Not too bad," he allowed. "How are things with the princess?"

Brown had crossed paths with Princess Veronika of Lukinburg when she'd first visited the U.S., and it looked like the two of them were getting close. His fellow bounty hunters had ribbed him mercilessly about his obvious interest in the princess, especially after the latest development where he protected her from a kidnapping attempt…and temporarily appointed himself her reluctant bodyguard.

His friend made a snorting noise. "Don't you have anything better to do than poke into my private life?"

"It relieves the tension." Maybe because he was feeling bad about grabbing Courtney Rogers and kissing her, he took another shot at his friend. "Oh, come on, you can tell me if you got to first base with her."

Brown sucked in a sharp breath. "I don't tattle on royalty."

"That's a 'yes,' I gather."

Brown's voice changed. "I assumed you called to make a report. You got some problems?"

"Well, I almost got blown up an hour ago."

His friend drew in a sharp breath. "Care to explain that?"

"I don't have much time for jawing. You can get the details from the colonel. Can you put him on the line?"

"Sure."

A few seconds later his boss, Colonel Cameron Murphy, came on the line. "Joseph looked shook up. Everything okay out there?" he asked.

Riley clenched his hand around the cell phone. He might have started with the pit and the explosion. Instead the first question he asked was, "Did you know Courtney Rogers was pregnant?"

The colonel made a small sound. "I heard a rumor to that effect. It wasn't confirmed."

"Well, I'm confirming it," Riley said, hearing his own tone of annoyance.

"Is her pregnancy a problem?" Murphy asked.

"Not for me," Riley snapped. "But apparently it's set up an antagonistic situation with the prudish little town of Spur City."

"Like what kind of situation?"

Riley cleared his throat. "Someone took a shot at her a couple of days ago when she was driving from town back to the ranch."

Murphy swore.

"It could have been someone taking potshots at random cars and trucks. Or it could have been specifically directed at her. Either way, it complicates my assignment."

"Uh-huh," the colonel acknowledged. "Find out which."

"I intend to."

"So what about the explosion you mentioned to Brown?"

Riley gave him a brief account of the morning's fun and games.

Murphy whistled through his teeth. "Give me more details," he demanded.

Riley was about to answer when he heard a twig crack. "Gotta go," he said quickly, then pressed the end button.

When he stuck his head around the tree, he saw a man advancing on him—gun in hand.

It was Jake.

RILEY HELD UP HIS HANDS, palms out. "It's just me," he shouted. "Put down the gun."

Jake hesitated for a moment, then holstered the weapon. "What are you doing?" he demanded.

"Looking for some privacy. There isn't any in the bunkhouse. Or the barn."

"Privacy for what?"

"To call my mother."

Jake laughed. "You expect me to believe that?"

"Honest," Riley murmured. If you substituted Cameron Murphy for Mom. And he was kind of like a mother hen to the Big Sky guys—in a strictly military way, of course.

"Your mother! Oh, sure. What did she have to say?" Jake challenged.

"She's glad I arrived safely at the Golden Saddle, and that I'm settling in. And she says that Great-Aunt Josephine's love life is heating up."

Jake stroked his chin. "That's interesting, because we don't have cell phone reception in the area."

"This phone has a special satellite hookup," Riley answered. "I got it so I wouldn't be out of touch with Mom."

Or course, he didn't add that Big Sky was paying a lot more for the communications equipment and access than a ranch manager could afford.

Calmly he held out the instrument. "Too bad about the reception around here. Do you have anyone special you want to call? I always end up with lots of minutes left over. So if you want to make a call, you're welcome to the phone."

The ranch hand considered the offer. "No, that's all right," he answered offhandedly, but Riley knew he was still suspicious.

"So, did you want to talk about something?" he asked.

Jake shifted his weight from one foot to the other. "You rode out. Ms. Rogers followed you. Then I heard an explosion. I was about to saddle up and see what happened out there when you both came back. But you didn't say anything. What in the name of Sam Hill happened?"

Riley decided to play the scene differently than he had with Kelly. "How do you know it was an explosion? It could have been a jet plane breaking the sound barrier."

"We don't get military jets out here." He scuffed his foot against the ground. "And I was in the army in Korea. I know what an explosion sounds like."

Riley considered his options. Did Jake have something to do the "accidents"? Or was he genuinely worried?

"I rode out to have a look around the ranch—and found an old cabin in the bush," he said, watching the man carefully. "About three miles northwest of here. You know the place I mean?"

"Yeah."

"I dismounted to have a look. When I got halfway across the open ground between the cabin and the woods, I found out someone had rigged a bomb to go off like a Fourth of July rocket."

The older man looked him up and down. "You don't look any the worse for wear. You sure you're not pulling my leg?"

"I've got military training, too. As soon as I stumbled over the trip wire, I hit the ground."

Jake shook his head. "Mrs. Rogers didn't say anything about it when she came in."

"I thought we should keep it to ourselves."

"Why?"

"That might be the best way to figure out why the cabin was rigged to blow up."

"You think someone who works here would do that?"

"I don't know." He took off his hat and ran a hand through his hair, doing a good imitation of a man who's stepped into a situation he doesn't much like. "I just took this job at the Golden Saddle three days ago. I'd like to keep my hide in one piece while I'm here."

"Are you fixin' to leave?" Jake demanded.

"Do you want me to?" Riley shot back.

They regarded each other in edgy silence.

Finally Jake answered, "I don't know. I'm still trying to figure out if I trust you."

"What would I be up to? If you don't mind my asking."

Jake waited another moment before answering, "There are people in town who want Mrs. Rogers to clear out."

"Just because she's pregnant and unmarried?"

Jake's face contorted. "It might be more than that."

"What else?"

"She's renting a piece of her property to guys some people don't like." He cleared his throat. "Some kind of militia group."

"What do you know about them?"

"Nothing. A long time ago, I decided the best way to get on in the world was to mind my own business. I just know one of them came here and signed a lease. That's all."

He was obviously saying as little as possible. And Riley figured that making a big deal out of the militia might put the old guy on the alert. So he simply nodded.

CROWN PRINCE NIKOLAI PETROV wiped his mouth delicately on a napkin and pushed his chair back from the table. He was in a Montana hotel, eating a solitary, room-service meal. His own company suited him perfectly.

The food was much too bland for his tastes. And the ingredients were inferior. But he was willing to put up with it, because his lecture tour through the American hinterlands was an important part of his mission to spread the word about his country, Lukinburg, to the American people. The U.S. had sent forces to the former Soviet satellite country to help overthrow the repressive government of his father, King Aleksandr. And he wanted to make sure the troops stayed there as long as necessary.

Which meant winning the hearts and minds of the American people.

So he had an ambitious schedule of public appearances in towns and cities across the continent. A smile flickered across his well-shaped lips. He knew from the e-mails and letters he had received and from the press reports that he was making a good impression on the population. Especially the women. He had no modesty about his sex appeal. He knew it helped his political cause to be young and trim with movie-star looks. And it didn't hurt that he'd been educated in one of their top Ivy League Schools.

Moving to the desk, he picked up the tablet he'd been writing on. His next speech would be in four days. And it must be as good as he could make it—even with the added burden he'd placed on himself with the composition of these talks.

Each word was important. And he couldn't turn the task over to a paid speech writer. This had to be done personally—his personal mission to the American people—making them think about the political situation in Lukinburg.

He chuckled at the thought—then got down to work in earnest.

Chapter Seven

The next day the garage brought back Courtney's truck. She checked it out, then retreated into the house.

Since she planned to take Riley's advice, she changed into something more comfortable—one of the softly flowing maternity dresses that she liked to wear when she got the chance.

The loose-fitting dresses were an indulgence. But she enjoyed the flow of the soft fabric against her skin—and liked the feeling of femininity they created.

Outside, her life was all hard surfaces and rough, men's work. In the house she could relax and let her hair down.

Drifting to the window, she gazed toward the barn. Riley was talking to Jake.

From her vantage point, it looked like her oldest hand and her new manager weren't getting along too well. It would be unfortunate if they couldn't settle down and work together. But you never knew how Jake would take a newcomer. If he'd been younger, she would have asked him if he wanted the ranch manager's job. But she'd known it would be too much of a burden for him. And she hadn't shared her reasoning with him— for fear he'd be insulted if she mentioned his age.

She took her bottom lip between her teeth. Had she done the wrong thing? Had she made him feel that she was shoving him aside when she'd started searching out a replacement for Ernie?

Courtney sighed and turned away from the window. Sometimes she felt as if the ranch was too big a responsibility for a woman alone. If she felt that way when she was pregnant, how would it be when she had a child to take care of? She'd have a whole lot more to do. If Riley didn't work out, she was up a creek without a paddle.

And right now she was in trouble in ways she had never anticipated. Someone had shot at her from the bridge. Then a cabin had blown up yesterday. She didn't know why. Or who had done it. Or if the incidents were connected.

She shuddered. Were the two events part of a pattern? Or were they separate? And which alternative was worse?

She had no answers. About the cabin or the shooting.

Or about Riley Watson, either. Unfortunately, she was attracted to him. But that attraction could go nowhere. Not in her present circumstances. Her getting involved with her ranch manager wouldn't be fair to him. Or the baby. She couldn't get wound up in a new relationship when her attention should be focused on her child.

Better to think about something besides the way Riley's hard body had felt pressed to hers. In bed—and after he'd clambered out of that horrible trap.

She should be thinking about Edward…not Riley. He'd been her husband. And he was the father of her child.

She and Ed had met in college in Billings, where they had both majored in ancient history. She'd been fresh off the ranch, but she'd loved the atmosphere of the university. They'd shared a passion for reading historic documents written in the original languages. That's what had brought them together in the first place. They'd both been after the same reference book and realized they'd have to share it.

Her hand slipped down to her abdomen, and she pressed her fingers over the bulge where Ed's baby was growing inside her.

They'd been sure they were in love—even though her parents had tried to warn her that she and Edward Rogers were too different to make a relationship work. She hadn't wanted to hear it. But they'd been right.

During their marriage, her husband had been away so much that she'd gotten used to being without him. Now sometimes it was hard to believe he was really dead—and not just on another one of his long assignments.

"But if you'd known people were shooting at me, you would have come back to help, right?"

She snapped her mouth closed. There was no point in talking to Ed or wishing he were here to defend her. He wasn't here. But Riley Watson was.

Yesterday, she'd kissed him. Somehow they'd grabbed each other like two shipwreck survivors who had finally spotted land.

Or had she led him on? Did he know from the previous afternoon in the motel that she'd welcome his advances?

Damn, she had to know what she'd done in that motel room. Because the gap in her memory was driving her crazy. And the tension couldn't be good for her or little Emily. Or maybe the name should be Hannah.

A knock at the door made Courtney jump. Pulling aside the curtain, she looked out and goggled at the man standing on the front porch.

Speak of the devil. There was Mr. Watson, looking as sinfully tempting as he had in that motel room.

Don't think about how good he looks, Courtney ordered herself. *You hired him to work for you. You have to keep your relationship businesslike. That's best for everyone concerned.*

"Just a moment," she called out, then hurried down the hall.

When she opened the door, she might have been tempted to talk on the porch to keep Mr. Watson out of the house, but the blast of cold winter air sent a chill across her skin.

"I guess you'd better come in," she said, thinking she sounded rather ungracious. Lord, why couldn't she seem to strike the right balance with the man?

Either she was clasping him in her arms or pushing him away.

The first image made her face heat, and she turned quickly on her heel.

Her new ranch manager closed the door carefully behind him, keeping his back to her for a moment. Finally he turned around to face her. But he said nothing, and she was very aware of how she must look. Before, he'd only seen her in one of the man-size shirts she wore over a pair of maternity jeans.

Now she knew her blue jersey dress was clinging to her breasts and to the swell of her abdomen.

As she pictured what she must look like, she felt as big as a blue whale, and she wished she'd dressed in one of her usual outfits.

He was speaking, and she fought to focus on his words.

"I've inspected your spread, and I do have some questions about the ranch."

She'd always invited Ernie into the kitchen or the office when they talked about ranch business. It made sense that she should do the same with Riley, although she simply didn't feel as easy with him. And it seemed like he wasn't any too comfortable with her, either.

Still, she heard herself saying, "Can I get you a cup of tea?" The moment the words were out of her mouth, she flushed. She'd always offered Ernie coffee. But since she'd found out she was pregnant, the smell upset her stomach. "Probably you don't drink tea," she said, then felt even more foolish.

"Tea would be fine," he answered.

In the kitchen, she busied herself filling the kettle, then setting it on a burner, aware that he was watching her.

"What did you want to ask?" she said quickly. "I mean, about the ranch."

"I've been making a list of possible improvements. You need to do some work on your access road before one of your vehicles breaks an axle."

She winced. "I know."

"I take it you don't own a grader."

"We used to have a small one. It's not operational. I'd have to rent one—and money has been pretty tight."

"Well, we need to squeeze it into the budget."

She answered with a tight nod, because she knew he was right. The kettle whistled, and she snatched it off the burner, then got down mugs.

"I'm glad you followed my advice—about staying in the house, I mean."

"There wasn't anything that needed my attention outside," she answered, knowing she sounded diffident.

She wanted to tell him that she could take care of herself. But she knew he was right about being careful. If staying inside helped keep the baby safe, then she'd do it.

Maybe he sensed her tension, because he changed the subject by saying, "I need to have some idea of your monthly expenses. And your income."

She stirred a teaspoon of sugar into her mug. "I sold three colts two months ago. They both had excellent bloodlines, and they both fetched good prices."

The conversation ground to a halt. She felt the weight of the silence between them and knew she had to clear the air. Before she could stop herself she said, "That afternoon in the motel room, I was pretty out of it." She cleared her throat. "I need to know—did I do anything improper while...while we were in bed together?"

When she heard his breath catch, she felt her face go hot. Damn, she knew it. He'd been keeping something from her—something that would embarrass her.

As he spoke, it was difficult for her to focus on the words. But she realized he wasn't confirming her worst fears. "You didn't do anything out of line." He shifted in his seat. "If anyone was tempted, it was me."

"How could you be tempted by a woman who's fat and ugly?"

He answered with a bark of laughter. "Is that how you think of yourself?"

"Yes."

"You're so wrong. I would have thought you'd figured that out after you helped me get out of that hole in the ground."

The statement hung in the air between them. She'd brought up the afternoon in the motel room.

He'd just added the incident from yesterday. And probably they both wished they'd keep their mouths shut.

"Maybe I'd better go look at your books," he said.

"Right." She jumped up so quickly that she made the mugs on the table rattle. "Let me show you the office.

"The account books are in the top-right-hand drawer of the desk," she said as he followed her down the hall. "Why don't you have a look at them, then ask me any questions that you have."

"That would be fine."

WHEN COURTNEY LEFT the room, Riley breathed out a small sigh. To put it mildly, he had found her presence distracting.

Easing open the desk, he found several old-fashioned leather bound books. If this was how she kept her accounts, he probably should convert the system to computer. Except that he wasn't going to be here very long, he reminded himself. He was only staying until Big Sky collected its bounty on Boone Fowler.

He listened hard for sounds from the hall. Then, because it was part of his assignment, he began opening other desk drawers, looking for anything incriminating.

He wasn't sure what that might be. He only knew he hated going behind Courtney Rogers's back.

But he had a job to do, he told himself grimly as he stared at a copy of her husband's death certificate, then the record of a five-thousand-dollar CD she'd cashed in recently.

When he felt uncomfortable enough, he put away the personal papers and began paging through lists of expenditures—then notations of payments.

As she'd said, she had made some money selling colts—and also on stud services for two of her stallions—who were apparently in demand among local ranchers.

There was also a notation for rent payments of $5,000 a month. Quite a hefty sum. If Boone Fowler could afford that much, he must be getting some serious financing. And the money was an important part of Ms. Rogers's current finances.

Well, the payments gave him an opportunity to bring up the "survivalists" again. And he had another idea, too. He'd been thinking that Courtney's problems came from people in town who were either upset by her unmarried-pregnant status—or upset because she'd allowed the militia to use her property. But suppose there was another motive? Suppose someone had decided her land was valuable—and they'd like her to quit the ranch, so they could take it over. He should ask her if anyone had made her an offer for the property. And he should ask the colonel to dig into the subject, as well.

No—scratch that. He had to stay focused and remember that his assignment wasn't to solve Courtney Rogers's problems. It was to make contact with Boone Fowler and his gang of thugs and find out what they were up to.

A noise from the doorway made him sit upright so quickly that he almost lost his balance.

Courtney stared at him from the doorway. "Are you all right?"

He shuffled the papers on the desk. "We should talk about your books."

"Do you have any problems with what you saw?"

"Nothing major, although your cash flow is pretty minimal."

"I know," she said quietly, then cleared her throat. "What if we talk about it over dinner."

Before he could stop himself he said, "I'd like that." In the next second, he wondered if he was out of his mind. He should be figuring out how to keep his distance, not sitting down for a meal with Ms. Rogers.

"Six o'clock," she said, as though she sensed he might change his mind.

"Yes. Thanks. I, um, wish I could bring something."

"No need," she said briskly, and fled the room.

"I'M HAVING DINNER with Mrs. Rogers," Riley told Jake when he came back to the bunkhouse.

The older man looked him up and down. "She invited you?"

"Yes," he answered, feeling as if he was checking in with a parole officer.

At five after six, all washed up and wearing his best pair of jeans and Western shirt under his coat, he stepped out into the frosty night.

As he strode across the ranch yard to the main house, he wondered if the knot in his stomach would ease up enough for him to eat. But the moment he caught the scent of roast chicken and dumplings coming from the kitchen, he felt his mouth water.

"That smells delicious," he told Courtney.

"Good."

While he shrugged out of his coat, she turned and hurried back to the kitchen.

She was wearing the same dress she had that afternoon, with a big apron tied around the front, emphasizing the small bulge at her middle.

She looked good enough to eat, and he forced himself not to stare.

OUT IN THE DARKNESS, Jake watched the couple in the kitchen. All cozy and nice. What a sweet domestic scene.

What the hell was Watson doing having dinner with her? She hardly knew him. There were guys on the spread—like him—who had been here since forever. Yet Watson was the one getting the nice little dinner.

Jake cursed under his breath. He'd come outside to check up on the dinner party. But he'd better get back where he belonged before someone saw him.

Still, he couldn't leave yet. He couldn't tear his eyes away from the lighted interior of the kitchen.

He stood there in the cold and dark for another few minutes, thinking of ways he could make life difficult for Watson and how he could let Courtney Rogers know that she was making a mistake.

She was seven months pregnant. Now she was playing house with Watson?

Jake snorted. He didn't like this turn of events much. Too bad that explosion out at the line cabin hadn't taken care of Watson.

But it was only a matter of time. The guy would make a bad mistake—and Jake would have him by the short hairs.

SCRAMBLING TO KEEP his mind focused on his real job, Riley asked, "So what do you think about the political situation in Lukinburg?" Immediately he wondered if Courtney was going to think that was a damn odd question.

But she seemed glad to give him her opinion. "I used to be for the war. But my...husband was killed over there. So I started rethinking our involvement in the sovereign affairs of another country. "

"Oh."

"But I do admire Crown Prince Nikolai—and the way he's stood up to his father's tyrannical government. He's a very eloquent advocate for his people."

"Um," Riley answered with another brilliant rejoinder. He would have liked to keep probing, but he didn't want to seem too interested in Lukinburg.

She turned off a burner under a bubbling pot. "Do you mind if we serve ourselves from the stove?" she asked. "That way I don't have to wash serving dishes."

"That's fine."

They busied themselves getting roast chicken with roasted vegetables and green beans.

After he'd taken a bite of tender chicken he said, "This tastes wonderful."

"It's just a simple meal."

"You're a great cook."

She flushed, then changed the subject abruptly. "Tell me about yourself."

"There's not much to tell. I grew up on a small ranch in Texas. My mom was the ranch cook."

"Then I'm bush league compared to her."

"Hardly."

"What about your dad?"

"He disappeared from the picture when I was just a kid."

"I'm sorry."

"Mom tells me we were better off without him. And instead of one dad, I had a whole ranch full of substitute fathers."

"Was it a good boyhood?"

"Basically."

"And that's where you got your first ranch experience?"

"Yeah. I learned to ride and rope—and take care of the stock. I rode a bronco in my first rodeo when I was fifteen." He laughed. "And I ended up on my butt in the dirt."

"Did you work at that ranch? I mean…for pay. Then go on to other spreads?"

"Mmm-hmm." He shifted in his seat, uncomfortble with being forced to lie to her face.

"So you like ranch life?"

"Yeah," he answered, hoping she hadn't caught

the emotion in his voice. He liked it all right—especially here with her. "What about you?"

"I could have moved away. But this land is part of me. Five generations of my family have lived here."

He envied that sense of belonging. To shift away from the personal discussion, he asked, "So, with regard to your books, you're relying pretty heavily on the rent those survivalists are paying you."

"Yes," she said quietly. "We signed a one-year contract, with an option for renewal."

"That's a long commitment."

"The leader, Boone Fowler, said it wouldn't be permanent."

"What do you know about him?"

"Not much. But I know that I need the money!" she said, in a voice that warned him not to pursue thesubject.

So was she upset because she didn't want to consider cutting off an important source of income? Or because she was in sympathy with the militia?

When he put down his fork, she said, "I've got cookies for dessert."

"I don't need any."

"But I can use you as an excuse to have some myself."

"Sure."

She gave him an apologetic grin. "To avoid temptation, I put them where I couldn't reach them without going to considerable trouble."

"I can get them for you."

"No need. I'm accustomed to doing for myself," she answered briskly. Getting up, she walked quickly to the pantry, coming back with an old step stool. Before he could stop her, she was climbing up on it and reaching into one of the upper cabinets.

Maybe she was nervous. Maybe she wasn't used to the roundness of her body. Or maybe she was reaching too far to the side. But as she climbed to the top of the stool, it wobbled and slipped from under her. And she screamed in surprise and panic as she fell.

Chapter Eight

Riley sprang out of his chair so fast that it fell backward and crashed onto its back.

His heart was pounding as he leaped across the space separating him from Courtney and caught her as she was coming down.

She crashed against his body, but at least she stayed upright as he lowered her feet gently to the floor.

She clung to his shoulders, swaying on unsteady legs, and his arms automatically tightened around her as he thought how fragile she felt in his embrace.

"Lord, you scared me," he breathed. "When I saw you tumbling through the air, my heart stopped."

"I scared myself." She pressed her face to his shoulder. "You move fast. I mean, it wouldn't have been a big deal, except for the baby."

"Yeah."

"I guess putting the cookies up there wasn't the brightest thing I ever did."

"Are you all right?" he asked, the question coming out in a little wheeze.

"Yes. Thanks to you."

Now was the time to set her away from him. But he didn't want to let her go. And she seemed to have no inclination to move, either.

The last time he'd held her, they had both been wearing heavy coats. Now she was dressed in a clinging knit shift through which he could feel every sweet curve of her body—her breasts, the slightly rounded swell of her tummy, the sweet seduction of her hips. He had to stiffen his arm to keep from lowering his hand to her bottom, so he could press her more firmly against himself.

His breath turned ragged. "Courtney?"

She didn't move, didn't stir. When she raised her face to his, her skin was beautifully flushed.

His mouth hovered less than an inch over hers, and it felt as if time stood still. Silent messages seemed to pass between them.

Can I kiss you again?

You know you can.

She slid her hand up, clasping the back of his hair and tugging him gently toward her. He lowered his head, bringing his mouth to hers.

This time, he had vowed that he would be gentle. But the moment their mouths touched, something hot and frantic bloomed between them.

His lips moved over hers. And he heard a low sob well up in her throat.

Her hands roved restlessly across his back and shoulders, as though frantic for contact. And his hands stroked over her in the same restless rhythm.

They rocked together, clinging, as the kiss turned more hungry. It was hard to think with the blood pounding through his veins and pooling in the lower part of his body.

He had been without a woman for months. When he'd come out of that prison camp, he had thought of himself as unfit for female companionship. He wasn't sure what he thought now. He just knew that touching Courtney, kissing her, was like a feast.

He needed more, so much more. Without thinking, he eased far enough away to slide one hand between them. He shouldn't take liberties. But he couldn't stop himself from gently stroking the side of her breast.

He was ready to pull his hand away if she objected. But the small sound she made in her throat was no objection.

The hand moved to cup her, then his index finger stole upward to find her nipple. It was erect, begging for his touch. And when he stroked the finger across the hardened nub, she moaned into his mouth.

"Oh, Courtney."

She answered with his name. He was so tuned to her that the world had contracted to a small bubble—with space for only the two of them. The atmosphere inside the bubble was punctuated by breathy exclamations and small sighs.

He felt as though they were the only people in the world. He moved back against the kitchen counter, taking her with him, splaying his legs to equalize their heights. She leaned against him, her sex pressed to his erection. And he closed his eyes, drifting on a current of sensuality.

Suddenly, a sound penetrated his consciousness, and he was instantly alert.

"Riley?"

There was no way to ignore his training. He thrust Courtney away from him.

She blinked up at him, her eyes registering confusion—and hurt.

"The front door!"

The words were barely out of his mouth when an angry-looking man strode into the kitchen. A man with a gun drawn.

Courtney gasped.

Riley struggled with an overwhelming sense of déjà vu.

It was Jake with a pistol in his hand. Again.

Hadn't they been through this yesterday?

"What the hell is going on?" the ranch hand demanded.

"I could ask you the same thing," Riley shot back. "How come every time I turn around, I trip over you?"

Courtney stared at the new arrival, then added her question to the tension in the room. "Jake? What are you doing? Put that gun away."

He looked reluctant. Yet he did as she asked. "I...I heard you scream," he said.

"What...did you think that I was attacking her?"

The man's face told Riley he did—or he was using it as an excuse.

Courtney stepped into the breach. "I fell off the step stool," she said firmly, pointing to the stool lying on the floor. "And Riley kept me from landing on the floor."

"Are you all right?" Jake asked immediately. Riley saw that Courtney's eyes were bright and her cheeks flushed. He didn't want to speculate on what *he* looked like. But he could feel the skin of his face stretched taut over his cheekbones.

He turned away and picked up the stool. When he set it on its feet, one of the legs wobbled, and he stooped down to examine it more closely.

"What's wrong?" Courtney asked.

"This leg is loose."

She looked perplexed. "It was fine the last time I used it."

"Well, it's not fine now," Riley snapped, tension and embarrassment making his voice sharp. "Who's been in here?"

He looked from her to Jake.

She shook her head. "Nobody!"

"Can you remember the last time you used the stool?"

"A few days ago. To get down some bathroom cleaner. I've put it up high—to get ready for the baby."

"And the baby is the issue now," he reminded her. "A seven months' pregnant woman falling from that height could be in big trouble."

She blanched and pressed her palm against her middle.

"Has anyone else been in here while you've been home?"

"Just you," she murmured.

Which made it hard to pinpoint when it had been tampered with—if it had.

She hurried on. "But it's old. Maybe it just gave out."

"Maybe," Riley muttered, wondering if it was true. What if one of her hands had loosened the leg? Or some guy had sneaked over from the militia camp? He wanted to say he'd spend the night in her living room—making sure nobody got into the house. But he was sure she wouldn't go for that. Straightening he said, "I should be going."

Jake made an identical observation.

Without waiting for further comment from Courtney, Riley strode down the hall, grabbed his coat and headed back to the bunkhouse.

The other men were watching a video in the living room. He saw that it was *The Horse Whisperer.* A story set on a horse ranch in Montana. Talk about a busman's holiday, he thought.

So was one of these guys a traitor?

"How was dinner?" Billy Cramer asked.

"Good."

"You look like something didn't agree with you," Kelly observed.

Once again Riley could imagine the look on his face, but he denied that anything was wrong. "No. I'm just tired. I had a big day."

He listened for the sound of Jake's footsteps. Either he was still over at the main house—or he'd gone for a walk. But he would be back at the bunkhouse sometime soon.

Riley hesitated. He could have joined the other men and pretended to be sociable. Instead he strode into his own room and closed the door.

It was obvious that Jake had been spying on him. And he'd heard Courtney scream. But he'd waited a couple of minutes before coming in with his weapon drawn.

So did that mean he'd been watching the romantic action through the window? Or was he waiting to catch Riley in the act of—what?

Was he anxious to save his boss from getting ravaged and make her grateful? Or did he have another motive?

The last time Riley had called into base, he should have asked Big Sky to investigate the man. Maybe he would have, if Jake hadn't appeared with his gun that first time.

Well, one thing Riley knew for sure—he was going farther from the house the next time he called Big Sky.

He sighed. Making a decision about using the phone was easy. But he knew he sure as hell hadn't been thinking a few minutes ago.

Courtney had ended up in his arms…again. And he recognized that his feelings for her were getting rapidly out of control. Hell, he was thinking about her more than Boone Fowler.

He'd had a sweetheart back in high school. He'd thought they'd get married and settle down—with him working as a horse trainer. But he'd wanted to save some money, so he'd joined the army. When he'd gone off to basic training, she'd started dating another guy. That had been a crushing blow. At first he'd been wary of getting hurt again. Then he'd decided that keeping his relationships with women casual freed him from obligations and allowed him to take jobs where he was on the move—and in danger. Ed Rogers had taken the same kind of jobs. Only, he'd had a wife waiting for him at home. How could the guy have done that? He knew how *he* felt about Courtney.

She brought out all the protective, tender instincts that he'd kept under wraps. Now he was sorry he'd rushed into his room, because he wasn't exactly in the mood to be alone with his thoughts. On the other hand, he couldn't picture himself sitting around with Jake and the other guys this evening.

So he took off his clothes and climbed into a cold bed—which helped cool him down.

RILEY WANTED TO STAY around the ranch yard, watching the men for signs of deviant behavior. But he needed to contact Big Sky. So he saddled Monty and rode out from the ranch, taking a more southerly direction than he had previously. This time he was going to ask them about Jake. And he was going to make sure he wasn't interrupted.

His plans changed abruptly when he heard the sound of automatic weapons fire. He reined in the horse quickly, thankful that his mount took the unexpected noise in stride.

Tying the horse to a tree, he dismounted and started moving through the woods—figuring that he must have finally found Boone Fowler and his gang of thugs.

He'd come to the ranch to make contact with Fowler. And he knew damn well he looked nothing like the sorry bastard who'd been in custody at the militia man's prison camp. Still, his pulse pounded in his ears as he moved cautiously through the woods, determined to make sure he didn't end up at the wrong end of the firing range.

He reached the edge of the clearing and stopped. He could see a line of guys dressed in fatigue outfits—firing at man-shaped targets.

They stopped shooting, and Riley was considering his next move when he heard the sound of raised voices. To his astonishment, he saw Courtney Rogers talking to a tall man with scrabbly hair and a scarred face.

Riley felt his stomach do a flip. Boone Fowler.

The man had obviously figured it was a good idea to change his appearance. He'd cut off his ponytail and shaved his beard. But there was no mistaking him. After being Fowler's captive, Riley would know him anywhere—even in a darkened room—because he would have recognized his stench.

Though he'd changed his appearance, the militia leader had obviously been too cocky to change his name. It was as if he felt untouchable and was thumbing his nose at the locals and the authorities, daring them to come after him...and live to tell about it.

The man wore sunglasses over his calculating dark eyes, but Riley could imagine the look he was giving Mrs. Rogers.

Fowler's attention was focused on her. What the hell was she doing here? She'd stayed in the house for the past few days. Now she was deliberately disobeying orders.

Riley edged closer, determined to pick up on the conversation—if he could do it without getting shot.

COURTNEY STOOD HER GROUND, even when such close proximity to Boone Fowler made her almost physically sick.

She'd told Riley that she'd rented some of her property to the man because she desperately needed the money. She hadn't wanted to admit that she'd come to question that decision.

This morning, when Billy Cramer had come to

the house to tell her he'd heard gunfire out on the range, she'd figured she'd better investigate personally. Of course, she could have turned the job over to her new ranch manager. But he'd never dealt with Fowler, and she knew it wasn't fair to send him into a confrontation with a man he'd never met.

So here she was, wishing fervently that she was somewhere else.

Clearing her throat, she said, "I didn't authorize you to use automatic weapons on my property. They are totally inappropriate on a ranch. Somebody could get hurt."

"I'm sorry, ma'am. That's part of the drill. I can't go over our practice schedule with you."

"And do you have to practice blowing up cabins?" she shot back.

"Yes we do."

"You told me you were opposed to the war— that you were a peaceful, survivalist organization."

He gave her a smile as fake as a three-dollar bill. "That's the Lord's honest truth, ma'am. But like everybody in this country of ours, we got to be prepared to defend ourselves." Giving her a direct look, he continued, "Folks have to take the initiative. Like, if public opinion had been against the war, then the U.S. would have been out of

Lukinburg by now. And your husband never would have gotten hisself killed over there."

Courtney answered with a brusque nod. The last thing she needed was this guy telling her that Edward might be alive if U.S. foreign policy had been different. She wanted to inform Fowler that if he didn't quit shooting machine guns and blowing up cabins, he was out of here. But she knew she had no way to back that up. He had a signed lease. She couldn't afford to hire a lawyer to break it. And sending her men up against these guys was out of the question—although she had the suspicion that Riley Watson was as tough as the militia leader.

She struggled to calm herself. She had her unborn child to think about, and getting into a fight with Boone Fowler might not be in Hannah's best interests.

He confirmed that assessment in the next moment. He'd been acting semireasonable. Now, before her eyes, his scarred face turned hard.

"What you'd better think about is that you rented property to me, and I have the right to use it any way I want."

"Not if somebody else could get hurt," she countered.

"Nobody's going to get hurt—if they stay clear of this area." His gaze dropped to her middle.

"That goes double for a lady with a bun in the oven."

She wanted to ask if he was threatening her. But she saw that all of his men had turned to watch the conversation.

She wanted to say she'd call the sheriff. But she knew that would do her a fat lot of good. Sheriff Pennington had already taken Fowler's side in a local dispute—when Tim Murch had accused Fowler's men of stealing a cow and butchering it. Why would the sheriff be any more likely to help her?

With as much dignity as she could muster, she turned and walked back toward the road where she'd left her truck, since she hadn't wanted to come this far on horseback.

She felt her breath catch and her vision cloud.

"Oh, oh…sugar," she muttered.

She needed another source of income besides these guys with an army arsenal. Maybe Riley Watson was right; perhaps she should invest in some cattle and train the horses to work them. But that would involve an outlay of cash. And more men. And she'd be gambling on making a profit.

By the time she was into the trees, tears were running down her cheeks. Angrily she swiped them away.

She wasn't some sissy. She had taken care of

herself for a long time—when her dad had been sick and then when Edward had taken those overseas assignments, leaving her alone more than he was with her.

A footstep behind her had her reaching for the gun she'd brought along and whirling awkwardly. Her body was starting to get in the way. She'd lost her balance last night, and she was in danger of doing it again. Cursing, she struggled to steady herself.

"Easy."

To her amazement, Riley Watson caught her and steadied her again.

"Put away the gun," he growled.

She did, still thinking he was the last man she expected to see out here. And the last man she wanted to see. Well, that wasn't quite true. She would have been more alarmed to see Boone Fowler following her.

But she wasn't sure how to face Riley. Not after what they'd been doing the night before. She'd invited him to dinner to talk business—and ended up in his arms again. For some very heated making out. And she had to wonder if that was what she'd been thinking about all along, since the business discussion had been pretty minimal.

"What…what are you doing here?" she gasped out.

"I was out for a ride, and I heard shooting. I wanted to find out what was going on."

She fervently wished she could hide her tear-streaked face. He hesitated a moment, then stroked his finger over her cheek.

When she made a small sound, he took her in his arms. The gesture was comforting, and she could tell he was being careful not to hold her the way he had the night before.

His hand stroked over her back, and she wished her coat wasn't in the way so she could feel his touch more intimately.

With an inward groan, she banished that thought immediately.

"That's your tenant?" he asked in a rough voice.

"Yes."

"I heard the way he was talking to you. Do you want to tell me about it?"

"Billy heard them shooting this morning and told me. I...I came out here to get Fowler to stop the target practice. Somebody could get hurt."

"Yeah."

"Then when we started talking, I could see it was dangerous to cross him."

"I think that's a fair assessment."

"What am I going to do?" she said, then hated the needy sound of her own voice.

"Let me help you."

"How?"

"Tell me what you know about Fowler."

"Not much. He came to me asking to rent the buildings out here that my dad built for a…a tourist camp. I figured it was a way to get some extra money."

"Did you investigate him?"

"I checked out his references, but that's as far as it went," she admitted. "In hindsight I realize that probably wasn't enough."

Riley gave Ms. Rogers a long look. Obviously she'd been too wrapped up in her own pressing problems to pay much attention to the local news after Fowler and his men escaped from prison. And since it had been months since the prison break, other headlines had now taken precedence—primarily the war in Lukinburg. No point in freaking her out with the truth now. "You should have hired a detective agency to check him out," he said, the advice coming out gruffer than he intended.

"I know that now. I knew it the moment I got a good look at him!" she said savagely. "But by then it was already too late."

Her anguished face made him back off. "Okay."

"But you think I'm stupid for getting myself into this mess," she demanded.

He didn't answer. He would have liked to tell

her they were both in a mess. But he kept silent on that point—because he had to.

Then he offered his own suggestion, playing fast and loose with the truth. "Maybe if I could get to know the guy, I could pick up some information you could use."

She raised large eyes to his. "You'd do that—for me?"

Again he was caught in the lie that Big Sky had forced on him.

"Yeah," he answered. "What do you know about his habits…his social activities?"

She looked thoughtful. "I guess he'd be suspicious of anyone who walked up and tried to say 'howdy.'"

He laughed. "Yeah.'" He forced his voice to remain casual. "I don't suppose you happen to know where he hangs out in town?"

She waited a beat, and he was afraid she wasn't going to answer. Then she said, "I hear he likes to let down his hair at the Grizzly Bear Bar."

"Maybe I can go there—and pick up something useful."

She looked as if she was sorry she'd shared the information. "I don't want you to get hurt."

"I won't," he said, then patted her on the shoulder like he was her uncle or something. "You go on home now."

"Are you patronizing me?" she demanded.

"No. I'm doing what's best for you," he said, hoping like hell it would turn out to be true.

"Okay, thanks."

She stood staring at him with those big eyes, and he wanted to ask what she thought about last night—about his kissing her, touching her. But he didn't have the guts to bring that up.

After several moments of silence, she turned and walked toward her truck.

He watched her leave, plans forming in his mind. He had taken advantage of Courtney when she was worried and off balance. He wasn't proud of that. Yet he told himself he was doing her a favor—getting Boone Fowler out of her hair. But he knew damn well she wasn't going to approve of the method. In fact, her estimation of her new ranch foreman was going to go down a couple of notches. Maybe that was for the best. At least it would give her a reason not to get involved with him.

Which was what he wanted. Right?

Chapter Nine

In for a penny, in for a pound, Riley thought as he pulled into a space on the street across from the Grizzly Bear Bar and ambled toward the door.

He gave the establishment a considering look, thinking it wouldn't win any prizes for ambiance. It was just a plain wooden building at the edge of Spur City, with a generic neon Open sign in one of the windows. And a hitching rail along the curb. At the moment no horses were tied up there. But the lot next door was full of vehicles—mostly pickup trucks and SUVs.

A handwritten notice on the door requested no bare feet and no spitting. Well, that was certainly high class. Just the kind of bar he figured a lowlife creep like Boone Fowler frequented.

Don't think of him like that, Riley cautioned himself. *You want to make friends with him.*

It had taken Riley two days to set up the scenario he had in mind. And he hoped everything was in place.

Last night he'd woken up in a cold sweat, knowing his mind had gone spinning back to Fowler's prison camp, dreaming of being held up by two men while a third punched him in the stomach.

He hadn't slept again. And before he'd left the ranch, he'd spent long minutes looking at his face in the mirror and comparing it to the memory of the gaunt, shaved-headed man who had staggered out of Fowler's prison camp.

Well, he was going to find out pretty soon if the militia leader connected Courtney Rogers's new ranch manager with that sorry guy.

Get it over with, Riley ordered himself, then pulled open the door and stepped inside.

He was immediately assaulted by the smell of cigarette smoke, sweat and beer.

On his overseas assignments, he'd been in some scuzzy bars around the world. This one scraped the bottom of the barrel.

A low buzz of conversation reached his ears. and over that the sound of an old Glen Campbell song on the jukebox.

He looked down at the floor. It appeared to be about as clean as a hog pen.

While he waited for his eyes to adjust to the

gloom inside the bar, he pictured Courtney's face when she heard the news about him tomorrow.

Warning himself he couldn't worry about that, he brought his mind back to the business at hand.

Squinting into the darkness, he saw an un-adorned room with a bar, several wooden tables and chairs and a row of booths along one wall. The decorative accents consisted of advertising signs from beer companies.

Men, mostly cowpokes and other ranch types were ranged around the room at the tables and at the bar. At ten in the evening there were no women. Perhaps some prostitutes would show up later.

The militia leader and some of his cronies were occupying one of the booths in the back.

Another man he recognized was at the bar. Stan Lewis, a guy who sometimes worked for Big Sky. According to the plan that Riley had outlined to the colonel, Lewis had flown into Billings the night before and come to Spur City.

Riley moved next to Lewis along the scarred wooden bar. Resting one booted foot on the rail, he waited to be served, hoping he looked casual when his heart was pounding like a tom-tom.

The barman appeared and looked him up and down before asking, "Help you?"

"What do you have on draft?"

From the short list, Riley selected a Coors, then bent over his glass, gulping a swig of the brew.

Smooth, Watson. Slow down.

He waited before taking a slow sip, then another, like a guy who can't afford a lot to drink but wants to enjoy the atmosphere of the bar.

Yeah, what atmosphere, he thought as he leaned against the sticky counter.

He kept up the performance, spilling a little of the beer on his shirt so he'd smell drunker than he was.

Taking his cue—which was Riley getting halfway through his second beer—Lewis said, "You from this one-horse town?" His tone was conversational yet had an edge of hostility.

"For the time being," Riley answered, downing more beer and turning slightly away from the other man like he didn't want to get into a conversation.

As Big Sky had planned on the phone, Lewis left him alone for a moment, then said, "So what do you think about this patch of paradise?"

"It's a place to work. It will do for the time being. When I'm tired of Spur City, I can move on."

"And in the meantime? What do you make, five dollars an hour?"

Riley grunted.

"Maybe you should join the army and ship out to Lukinburg."

"Now wait a damn minute. What the hell are you talking about?" Riley asked.

Lewis raised his voice. "The war in Lukinburg is a good idea. We need more guys over there. Not punching cows in this frozen piece of Montana."

"I'm not punchin' cows. I'm raising horses."

The buzz of conversation had stopped. People were listening.

"Same difference," Lewis muttered, then plowed ahead. "Either way, you'd be better off in Lukinburg."

"No way. The war is a mistake. I wouldn't stick my nose in there—even if they paid me a million dollars."

"You're a coward!" Lewis retorted.

Riley glared at him. "Hey, since you're so gung ho for this blasted war, why don't you enlist?"

Lewis scowled. "I tried but I didn't pass the damn physical."

Riley leaned over his beer mug, pretending he'd had enough of the chitchat.

"You're not listening," Lewis growled, reaching for him and spinning him around.

"Get your damn hands off me," Riley barked.

"Make me."

Guys around them backed away.

Lewis gave him an apologetic look, then slugged him on the chin—making the punch all too realistic, as far as Riley was concerned. How long had the guy been in here drinking, anyway? Or was he settling a secret grudge? Was that the real reason he'd agreed to take this assignment?

With a growl of rage that was only partly faked, Riley slammed back, giving Lewis as good as he'd gotten.

"Hey!" The shout came from the bartender, who reached across the bar.

Lewis and Riley moved away—out of range. The next thing he knew, they were rolling on the floor, breathing hard and trading punches, having no problem making the fight look realistic. Maybe he'd underestimated his need to let off steam.

He heard somebody shout, "Call the sheriff."

"Naw, let 'em fight. I bet on the ranch manager."

"Ease up, man," Lewis muttered, through pants of breath.

Riley tasted blood in his mouth. He was thinking they'd both had enough. But there was no way to simply back out—and have the desired effect.

He almost shouted out in relief when someone grabbed him by the shoulders and dragged him off Lewis.

Moments later, Sheriff Pennington came crashing through the door. "What the hell is going on?" the lawman demanded as people in the bar held Riley and Lewis away from each other.

"He started it," Riley sputtered, feeling blood from his nose dripping down his face. Somewhere in his mind he was staring at himself in disbelief, appalled that he had put himself in this position in a lowlife bar.

"No—he did," Lewis shot back.

"I think we'll settle this down at the jail," Pennington said as he snapped handcuffs on Riley, then Lewis.

The moment the cuffs closed around his wrists, Riley shuddered at the thought of being locked up like a caged animal again.

Boone Fowler, the man who had held him in captivity less than two months ago was across the room—watching him with a good bit of interest.

Did he know this man was his former captive?

Riley fought the sick feeling in his throat. But Fowler and his men only observed from the fringes—staying away from the center of excitement.

Several guys who might have been deputies or simply buddies of the sheriff muscled them out of the bar. The crowd followed, talking excitedly as he and Lewis were hustled into a police cruiser.

Riley focused his gaze straight ahead, contracting his field of vision, concentrating on making his emotions numb. The way he had in the prison camp.

None too gently, Pennington escorted them into the sheriff's office. "This is your first offense in town," he growled. "If you don't give me any trouble, I'll turn you loose in the morning."

"Yes, sir," he and Lewis mumbled, acting like the sorry drunks they'd played at the bar.

Although Pennington didn't officially book Riley, he led him to a cell and locked him in. It wouldn't have happened that way in any big-city police department. But Big Sky had been counting on the lax procedures in Spur City.

Riley washed his face in the small dirty sink in the cell, then lay down on a hard bunk. The blanket smelled worse than he did, so he folded it and laid it at the end of the bed. He might have tossed it on the floor, but he didn't want Pennington to come at him for disrespecting government property or anything.

Alone in his cell, it was impossible to hang on to the numbness he had manufactured. Suddenly he felt a terrible tightness in his chest and throat.

This isn't Boone Fowler's prison camp, he told himself. But he kept glancing toward the bars, half expecting the "survivalist" to come in, scoop

him up and haul his ass back to the militia compound—where he could finish what he'd started
a couple of months ago.

In the darkness, he cursed Cameron Murphy for
coming up with this particular plan to get Boone
Fowler's attention. What if it wasn't even effec-
tive, and he had to go back to square one? Which
was what—exactly? Riding over to the militia
camp to introduce himself?

Yeah, right. "I'm the jerk who made a fool of
himself in the Grizzly Bear the other night."

He lay on the bunk all night, strung tight as a
guitar string, somehow keeping himself from
freaking out. In his saner moments, he reminded
himself of why Murphy had picked him for this
assignment. He was the chameleon. The man who
could take on any persona. Which meant he had
the best chance of convincing Boone Fowler that
he'd make an excellent recruit.

Still, as the darkness outside the barred window
gave way to gray and then morning light, his tension increased. Could he really face Fowler without cringing?

Pennington came back around 7:00 a.m.

"There's someone waiting to see you," he said.

Riley got up, assuming it was Courtney and
sickened by the idea of her seeing him like this.

But when the sheriff led him into the office,

the militia leader was leaning comfortably against the desk.

The two men exchanged a meaningful look, and Riley suddenly got the feeling that Fowler was the one calling the shots in town.

The militia leader looked the prisoner up and down, and Riley waited to see a gun materialize in his hand.

Instead the man shifted his weight from one foot to the other, then drawled, "Howdy."

"Howdy," Riley answered, shocked that the man had used the very greeting he and Courtney had been joking about—and at the same time surprised that he was able to sound so damn normal.

"We should have a talk," Fowler said.

"Sure, what about?" Riley inquired.

"Why don't we go where we can get comfortable?"

Riley nodded, still not certain what was in store for him.

RILEY WATSON WASN'T the only person in the Big Spur area who spent a sleepless night.

One of Courtney's hands, Billy Cramer, had been in town that evening, and he'd come back to the bunkhouse with the exciting news that the new ranch manager was in jail.

Of course, Jake had immediately hotfooted it to Courtney's front door to inform her. He'd had an "I told you so" expression on his face. And it had been all she could do not to kick him out of the house.

But she forced herself to speak quietly, telling him that they shouldn't jump to conclusions.

"You fired that Carson guy when he got drunk in town," Jake argued.

"I know. But things are different now. I need a manager."

"He's not reliable."

"We don't know that."

"He can't handle his liquor. We damn well know that. He got sloshed—then got into a fight."

She nodded. "I want to hear his side of the story."

Jake shook his head and walked out.

Courtney tossed and turned all night, feeling the child inside her kicking and wondering if she'd have to fire Riley Watson in the morning. He'd seemed so competent and so caring. Now she was thinking that he was just another man who was going to let her down.

In the morning she dressed and drove to Spur City. She parked near the jail, then started to get out of her truck—just as she saw Riley coming out of the building.

When she saw that the man beside him was Boone Fowler, she gasped.

The windows were closed against the cold, and there was no way Riley could have heard her. But maybe he recognized her truck, because his eyes were drawn to the driver's window. When he saw her staring at him, he had the grace to flush. But he never broke his stride. Instead of pulling away from Fowler, he continued down the street with the militia leader.

And she was left sitting behind the wheel, coping with a terrible sense of betrayal. All she could think was that she'd trusted Riley Watson. She'd let him get close to her. And this was what she got for that trust.

Fowler had threatened her two days ago. Riley had offered to get some information about the guy. Now here he was strolling down the street with Fowler like they were best friends.

SOMEHOW RILEY KEPT his composure as he saw the sick look on Courtney's face. He wanted to break away and stride to the truck. He wanted to tell Courtney this was all a charade. But he couldn't risk having Fowler see that he cared anything about her.

So he kept walking, fighting the knot of barbed wire in his gut.

They headed down the street, with several of Fowler's men falling into step behind them.

"How about here?" the militia leader said.

Riley eyed the bar where he'd made a spectacle of himself the night before. "I need some food in me."

"Well, Tim, the guy who owns the bar, is a friend of mine. He'll fix you some eggs."

Riley walked stiffly as they approached the bar.

It seemed like the militia leader didn't recognize him. But this could all be an elaborate trick to capture him.

"Yeah, you were a sight," Fowler said, acting as though he thought Riley was embarrassed about the night before. Inside, he ambled toward the booth where he'd been sitting the night before, watching the action. Two of Fowler's men joined them.

When the barman came over, Fowler asked for a tomato juice and scrambled eggs for his friend.

The militia leader stared at Riley across the table, and he forced himself to sit calmly, pretending he had never been in this man's clutches.

"So why did you get a job with the widow Rogers?" Fowler asked.

"I needed the money."

"There are other ways to earn money."

"I know horses."

"You been on a lot of ranches?"

"Yeah," Riley allowed.

"I hear you're getting things straightened out at the Golden Saddle."

From whom? Riley wondered. "I hope so."

"So why did you cut loose last night?"

"A guy's got to let off steam once in a while."

Fowler chuckled. "That's the truth."

Riley's eggs arrived, and he took a bite. They tasted as bad as he'd feared. He chewed and swallowed, then said, "And I didn't like hearing that jerk defend the war."

"Yeah, the war is a damn shame. I was impressed that you stood up for your convictions."

"I'm new in town. So I don't have all the players straight yet. You and your guys are opposed to the fiasco in Lukinburg?"

"We downright hate it that America can't keep its nose out of a foreign squabble. We're dedicated to doing what we can to get us out of there."

"Like—what can you do?"

Fowler glanced around as though spies had their ears pressed to every wall of the seedy bar. "I don't want to talk about that here."

"Are you sure you want to talk about it with him at all?" one of the men asked.

"Why not?" Fowler growled.

The man shrugged. "We got enough guys in our unit now."

Riley tensed, wondering what would happen now.

Fowler glared at the man. "Are you questioning my judgment, Anderson?"

The man shifted in his seat. "No, sir."

"That's good. Because what I say goes."

The other man looked down at his hands, but not before Riley caught the anger on his face.

Fowler turned back to the would-be new recruit. "If you want to join my group, we can give it a shot."

"You mean—move out there with you?"

"No. I was thinkin' that you should stay at the ranch...for now so Ms. Rogers can keep giving you a paycheck."

"Good idea," Riley said, hoping his relief didn't show. He wanted information about the militia group, but he didn't want to leave the ranch. Courtney needed to be protected.

"If I need to contact you, can you tell me where your compound is?" Riley asked.

"Sure." Fowler drew him a crude map, showing a turnoff to the militia compound several miles up the road from the main ranch entrance.

"Appreciate it," Riley said.

"I'll be in touch," the militia leader answered.

Riley wanted to press for something more definite. He wanted to inquire about Fowler's financial backers. Unless the man had robbed a bank, somebody was fronting him a sizable amount of cash. But he didn't want to seem like he was probing for information. So he only said, "I hope you don't wait too long."

"We know where to find you."

"What if Ms. Rogers fires me?"

"I'm sure you can talk your way around a woman like her."

The snide way he said it and the smirk on his face made Riley want to sock him. But he kept his temper and chuckled. "Yeah. I'm not too shabby with the ladies."

"Well, take a shower before you do any sweet-talkin'. You smell like you've been in a jail cell all night—after rolling around on a barroom floor."

"I'll wash the stench off," he said good-naturedly. He left a few minutes later without finishing his breakfast, feeling like he'd jumped a mountain-size hurdle. It looked like he'd gained Fowler's confidence. But he wasn't going to count on anything. Not yet.

On the way out of town, he saw one of the militia men talking to the general store owner. Another was at the gas station, zipping into line ahead of another customer. Nobody objected, which made Riley wonder again how much power

Boone Fowler had in town. Were people afraid of him? Or were they on his side?

COURTNEY MIGHT HAVE TURNED around and gone straight home. But she didn't want to hear Jake say, "I told you so." Besides, now that she was in town, she might as well check on the order of oats that was supposed to come in.

She was still sick from seeing Riley with Fowler. But she tried to put him out of her mind as she drove to the general store. Another truck was in back of her all the way to the store. Was someone snooping into her business?

When she slowed, the driver sped around her. She couldn't see his face, because his hat was pulled low. And when she tried to read his license plate, she found it was smeared with mud.

All at once, she thought of the guy up on the bridge, and she felt her throat close.

Pulling up at the general store, she sat behind the wheel, breathing hard, telling herself that nothing had really happened. But she didn't honestly believe that.

Finally, with a sigh, she got out of the truck and almost bumped into Joan Craig, the woman who had been hired to run the battered-women's shelter.

"Courtney, how are you?" Joan asked, her voice full of concern.

"Good," Courtney managed, hoping she sounded convincing.

Joan nodded, then went on to a topic Courtneydidn't want to discuss. "I hear your ranch manager got into some trouble last night."

"Um," Courtney answered. Joan was one of the people in town who was still friendly. But that didn't mean she wanted to talk to her about Riley Watson.

The other woman picked up on her mood and immediately switched topics. "Are you going to the opening of the shelter?" she asked.

"I wouldn't miss it," Courtney answered sincerely.

She hadn't attended a social event since before Edward had died. But she'd been a big supporter of the battered-women's shelter, because she understood that a woman who had been abused needed all the help she could get. Including a safe environment in which to heal while she figured out where she went next with her life.

Joan beamed and lowered her voice. "We're having a distinguished visitor at our ribbon cutting."

"Who?"

The other woman's eyes twinkled. "I'm not at liberty to tell. For security reasons."

"Oh," Courtney answered, her mind grappling with that. "Security reasons—in Spur City."

"Oh my, yes. But I can say you won't be disappointed if you come. It's someone we're all interested in hearing."

"The prince?" Courtney pressed. Crown Prince Nikolai of Lukinburg had been in Montana giving a speech recently. And he had another one scheduled soon. Maybe he was willing to extend his stay a few days so he could lend his prestige to the center's opening. She knew he wanted to free his people. Perhaps his interest in social causes didn't stop with the borders of his country.

Joan just gave her a mysterious smile and repeated that she wasn't at liberty to give out details.

The women chatted for a few minutes. Then Joan said she had to get back to work, and Courtney went to check on her order.

She also stopped at the grocery store, looking behind her several times because she thought she saw the same truck. But when she headed out of town, no one seemed to be following her, and she breathed a sigh of relief.

Then, ten miles past the city limits, she saw a vehicle in her rearview mirror coming up fast. He must have been following at a distance, because he knew where she was going. And now he was making his move.

Damn, it was him. And she couldn't hold back

the dread that rose in her throat. Gritting her teeth, she got her gun from the glove compartment and laid it on the passenger seat. Then she sped up, making for the hills and a stand of rocks where she and some of the other kids in town had hung out as teenagers.

Driving faster than she should, she took several turns at dangerous speed until a hill hid her from the guy on her tail.

When she came to the rocks, she pulled off the road, knowing that the boulders would shield her in both directions—up and down the road.

Sitting with the engine running, she took the gun in her hand and waited to find out if the guy had fallen for her trick.

Chapter Ten

Courtney couldn't see the road, but she heard the pickup roar past. She was sure that the driver was bent on catching up with her.

She shivered and slumped down in her seat, so that her head was barely visible above the windows.

Hopefully the driver wouldn't realize he'd lost her until much later. She waited fifteen heart-pounding minutes. Then she pulled cautiously onto the road.

It was clear, and she made a run for the ranch, praying that she wouldn't see the guy again.

When she was almost home free, he came at her once more, this time roaring down the road in the other direction. But she turned quickly onto the ranch road, then drove onto the hard-packed ground beside it, figuring she could make better time if she stayed off the bumpy surface of the driveway itself.

The guy hesitated at the entrance to the ranch. To her everlasting relief, Kelly came galloping toward her. The guy in the truck apparently decided to cut his losses and turned around and roared back toward town.

Kelly pulled alongside her.

"What are you doing down here?" she asked her hand, hearing the strain in her own voice.

"We were waiting to find out what happened. Where's Riley?"

"I don't know," she snapped, wishing that her men weren't keeping up with the situation. But what could she expect? "There's feed in the back. I'll meet you at the barn."

After the supplies were unloaded, she drove across to the house and carried the groceries in, thinking that she should have taken Riley's advice and stayed home.

She wanted to tell him about the man who had followed her. Then she reminded herself she didn't even know if he planned to stay here.

WELL BEFORE HE REACHED the ranch, Riley pulled up at the side of the highway and dug out the special cell phone that connected him to Big Sky. The sheriff had taken it away from him the night before—but he'd returned everything in the morning. And he hadn't checked out the instrument.

Riley called the office, and the colonel answered on the first ring. Apparently he'd been waiting for his man in Spur City to check in.

"Did the scene in the bar go as planned?" he asked.

"Basically," Riley answered. "But I didn't much like spending the night in jail."

"I can believe that," Murphy said with feeling. He waited a beat before asking, "So…you impress Boone Fowler?"

"I think so."

"You don't sound too pleased."

"I'm sure Stan Lewis isn't too pleased, either," Riley growled.

"I take it the two of you let off some steam?"

"You could say that. Or you could say he earned his fee—the hard way."

Murphy laughed, then got back on message. "What did Fowler have to say?"

"He liked my stand on the war. And he acted friendly. I assume he wants to test me with some assignment before he invites me out to his compound."

"And you're sure he didn't recognize you?" the colonel pressed.

Riley dragged in a breath and let it out. "As sure as I can be. Of course, he could be stringing me along, but we'll see." He got out the map that

Fowler had given him. "The road to the militia camp is only a couple miles up the highway from the ranch entrance. Maybe you'd better keep it under surveillance."

"Will do. And we'll see if Fowler or his men are meeting with anyone in town. You did good work."

"Thanks," Riley muttered.

"I know this isn't easy for you. It wouldn't be for me, either."

"I'll handle it," Riley clipped out, wondering if Courtney was going to fire him when he got back to the ranch. "Do me one favor, though. Check up on her ranch hand named Jake Bradley. I want to know if there's anything suspicious about him."

He ended the transmission, then continued up the road. He realized he was going slower and slower to postpone the moment of his arrival. With a curse, he sped up.

WHEN COURTNEY HEARD the sound of a vehicle, she looked out to see Riley's SUV pulling up in front of the bunkhouse.

He got out and went inside. And she waited tensely to see if he'd come out again with his gear.

When he didn't, she thought she should go over there and tell him he was fired.

But she couldn't make herself follow through. Much as she hated to admit it, she needed him.

Still, she didn't want to have anything to do with him at the moment. So she stayed inside. First she put away the groceries. Then she walked around the house, checking to see if anyone had been here while she was gone.

She didn't think so. But she didn't like the feeling of needing to look for booby traps in her own home.

WHEN RILEY STEPPED into the bunkhouse, Billy was the only guy inside. He looked up in surprise. "What are you doing here?" he said stupidly.

"Getting back to work. After I wash off the jail-house stench."

"You look like you went ten rounds with Mike Tyson."

"Thanks."

The other man gave him a considering look. "You lose your cool like that often?"

"Not often. That should do me for a few months," he said over his shoulder as he headed for his room, where he shucked his dirty clothes and kicked them into a corner, then headed for the shower.

In the mirror he inspected his face. One eye was

black, and his lip was a little swollen. But he had all his teeth.

He was back on the job a half hour later. But he felt like he was walking around on a bed of ground glass. If he tipped one way or the other, he was going to fall and cut the hell out of himself. Which was too bad, since he was already in a fair amount of pain from the blows Stan Lewis had landed on his face and body.

He kept thinking that Courtney was going to come marching out of the house and tell him to collect his first and last paycheck and leave. But she stayed away.

Kelly caught up with him as he stepped into the barn.

"Problem?" he asked.

"Buttercup is acting restless."

"She's due to foal soon?"

"Uh-huh. She came into season early."

"Sometimes it happens that way." Riley walked over to her stall, talking to the chestnut-colored horse soothingly as he examined her teats. Not all horses leaked milk. But he saw colostrum— which was a good indication that she was close to delivery.

"Tell the other men. And we'll check on her every hour."

"She's likely to wait until tonight…when she's alone," Kelly pointed out.

"I know," he answered, wishing that the Golden Saddle had a closed-circuit TV system. But apparently the equipment had been too pricey for Courtney.

They had already moved Buttercup to the large stall at the end of the row. Glad of something constructive to do, Riley helped Kelly muck out the stall and add fresh dry hay. All the while, he spoke to Buttercup, telling her she was going to have a fine baby very soon.

By that evening the mare was pawing at the straw and pacing around in the stall. After a quick dinner, Riley went back to the barn. Even though the chance of her developing problems was slight, he also knew that if something unexpected happened, he'd have to deal with it quickly.

He set out a kit of items he might need. But since a mare could stop her labor during the first stage if she was disturbed, he spread a blanket for himself on a pile of straw outside the stall.

He'd gotten very little sleep in the past couple of days, and he must have dozed off. The next thing he knew, a strangled exclamation woke him. Staggering up, he crossed to the stall and found Courtney down on her knees beside the horse.

Buttercup was lying on her side, pushing, but

when he looked between her legs, he saw what Courtney had spotted—a red bag at the entrance to the birth canal. And he knew what it meant. Premature separation of the placenta.

"Lord, why didn't I call the vet..." she gasped.

"Because something like this is so rare," he answered, knowing that immediate action was critical because the foal's oxygen came from the placenta, and it was no longer attached to the uterus. If they didn't get the foal out of his mother fast, it would suffocate.

There was no time to panic.

"Talk to Buttercup. Tell her everything's going to be okay," Riley directed, even when he knew it might be a lie.

He had no time for false moves. Dashing out of the stall, he grabbed the scissors that he'd gotten ready—just in case. Courtney was bending over the mare, speaking soothingly to her.

"I should be the one to do it," she murmured.

"No. Let me. She trusts you. You can keep her calm."

Courtney answered with a tight nod, stroking Buttercup's face as she bent to whisper soft words.

Feeling an unexpected composure wash over him, Riley knelt down at the other end of the mare and used the scissors to open the placenta, being careful not to cut Buttercup.

"I'll help her deliver if she needs me," Riley murmured, keeping his voice low and even to avoid alarming the horse.

Buttercup pushed again. When he saw two feet emerge, the tension began to ease from his body.

"The foal's in the normal position," he said, then saw the head follow, with the ears slicked back against the skull.

"Thank God," Courtney breathed.

As Riley gently tugged, Buttercup pushed her baby into the world.

Both he and Courtney breathed sighs of relief as she turned and began to lick her colt. He raised his beautiful chestnut head and looked at his mother.

They kept working together, making sure the baby had no breathing problems and washing Buttercup's udders.

By the time the foal had stood and taken his first drink of colostrum, Riley was exhausted.

"Thank you," Courtney said.

"We made a good team," he answered. They had worked together well, and it had felt good.

But now that the crisis was over, he could see Courtney was wavering on her feet. "You need some sleep," he told her.

"I was about to make the same observation to you."

They stepped out into the frosty air of early morning. When he started back to the bunkhouse, she reached for his arm. "I want to thank you for being here. I mean it. That colt could have died. But you saved him."

"I was doing my job," he said stiffly.

"More than your job. You could have called in someone else hours ago. But you stuck with Buttercup—and with me," she said softly.

His own voice remained gritty. "I wanted to see it through."

"And now you need to sleep. We both do. If you go back to the bunkhouse, the guys will disturb you. So why don't you use one of the guest bedrooms in my house?"

He wanted to ask why she was being nice to him. Instead he glanced toward the bunkhouse, where a light already shone in the kitchen window.

Courtney followed his gaze. "You go on and get some sleep. I'll tell Jake what happened and where you are. The bed in the room at the end of the hall is made up."

He answered with a small nod. The two of them needed to talk. But he didn't have the stamina for that now. He was exhausted, and he knew that he needed peace and quiet.

So he accepted her offer.

He entered the main house, then went down to the end of the hall to a blue-and-yellow room. After closing the door and the curtains, he staggered into the shower to clean up.

He might have slept naked, but some of his brain cells were still working. When he opened the closet, he found some men's soft flannel shirts. He put one on, then piled his dirty clothing on the chair in the corner.

The double bed was cold, and he spent a few minutes shivering—until his body heat warmed the sheets. Before he knew it, he was sleeping soundly.

TEN HOURS LATER, Riley was still out cold. Obviously he was exhausted, so Courtney left him alone.

She'd tried to keep busy during the day. Now she sat down on the chair and took off her boots, then walked to her bedroom in her stocking feet.

She didn't want to look all soft and feminine when Riley finally woke up. But her maternity jeans were feeling confining. So she changed into one of her dresses, hoping he wouldn't think she was doing anything special for him.

She'd checked on Buttercup and her foal several times. Both mom and baby were doing fine. She'd asked the other men to check, as well.

Probably they were wondering what she and Riley were doing in here. The answer was nothing—but that would have to change.

They needed to have a serious talk. She'd been so angry and hurt that she'd wanted to tell him to leave. Then she'd seen that there might be some logic to the way he'd introduced himself to Boone Fowler. Establishing his credentials, so to speak.

Edward had told her stories about his exploits on some covert assignments. And that had gotten her wondering seriously about Riley Watson.

The guy he'd been fighting with hadn't been local. And he'd gotten out of town as soon as he was released from jail. So was he someone sent here to get into a bar fight with Riley?

That was a pretty elaborate scenario. And not very likely. Still, Riley wasn't exactly acting like a guy who was just a ranch manager—although he'd proved he knew horses last night.

She tiptoed down the hall, listening outside his door. When she heard a noise inside, she went still.

Riley groaned and shouted something.

Suddenly she thought about the guy who'd shot at her—maybe the same guy who'd followed her from town. Or the person who had broken the leg on her step stool.

Was he here—attacking Riley? Or was this

some kind of fallout from the fight in the bar two nights before.

Acting quickly, she turned the knob and pushed into the room.

The shades were drawn, but in the shaft of light coming from the hall, she could see Riley was alone in bed, his head thrashing on the pillow.

He called out again, and she stood transfixed as she heard him say, "You can do any damn thing to me you want, you bastard, but I'm not going to tell you squat. So you might as well put me back in solitary." He ground out the words, in a low, gravelly voice.

But his brave speech was followed immediately by a groan, and she was pretty sure he was reliving some horrible episode from his past. Lord, what had happened to him?

He made a harsh sound of pain, and she knew she had to bring him back to the present.

Quickly she crossed the room and bent over the bed, her long hair sweeping down in a curtain as she leaned over the sleeping man and touched his shoulder.

"Riley, wake up. You're having a bad dream."

She hadn't been prepared for his reaction. His hand shot out, grabbing her by the hair and yanking her down to the surface of the bed. Then his hands were around her throat.

She screamed, instinctively flailing at him with her hands and feet.

His grip tightened, cutting off her breath, and she felt a moment of blind, stark terror.

Riley, no! She screamed the plea in her mind, praying he could somehow hear her.

She heard him curse as the pressure on her windpipe eased abruptly.

"Courtney?"

"Yes," she wheezed.

"Oh, God, are you all right?"

"Yes."

She flipped her hair out of the way and saw the anguished look on his face.

"I'm so sorry. I thought…you…were the enemy." His voice was laced with pain. He started to heave himself out of the bed, then cursed again. "I'm not exactly dressed for company."

"You have on a shirt."

"But no pants."

"Oh," she said stupidly, then realized that while she had him off balance she might as well try to get some facts out of him.

"You were in a jail?"

"A prison camp."

"Overseas?"

"No," he said sharply, focusing on her. "Are you trying to pump me for information?"

"Yes," she admitted. "So tell me why I came to get you out of the pokey and found you with Boone Fowler."

"He was being friendly. I figured I'd get to know him."

"Just because you want to help me?"

He looked down at the blanket. "I wish youwouldn't keep asking questions."

"Because you hate lying to me."

"Yes."

"But you've been doing it, anyway."

"Yeah."

She turned her head away and started to get off the bed. His hand shot out and circled her wrist.

"Wait."

"Give me a reason why I should stay."

In the darkened bedroom he dragged in a breath and let it out. "Because the idea of your hating me is intolerable."

When she hesitated, he went on in a low voice. "Getting into a bar fight over the war and getting my ass arrested was a great way to meet Fowler. But being in jail the other night made me flash back to prison camp. Being in a cell. Being under someone else's control. That's why I had the nightmare."

"Oh, Lord, Riley. I'm so sorry."

She heard him swallow. "Let me hold on to you."

The way he said it made her feel like he was the needy one. Wondering if she was making the biggest mistake of her life, she eased back onto the mattress. She could feel herself trembling, perhaps from the cold.

He must have felt it, too, because he pulled aside the covers. "Get under," he said gruffly.

"We both know I shouldn't. Especially when I can't trust you."

"I think I proved I can behave myself in bed."

"I'm not just talking about now. I'm talking about the big picture."

"Get under the covers, and we'll figure that out later."

It was an outrageous suggestion. He was taking liberties with her emotions. Maybe he was even trying to manipulate her. And if she knew what was good for her, she should get up and leave the room as fast as she could.

Chapter Eleven

To Courtney's amazement, she did as he asked. Maybe she was living in a fairy tale. Maybe she wanted to forget the weight of responsibility resting on her shoulders—at least for a little while.

Closing her eyes, she lay down beside him.

"Thank you," he breathed as he gathered her into his arms.

She snuggled into his warmth and his scent. Once before, he had held her in his arms in a bed, but she knew this time was different. Back then, they hadn't known each other. Now they had been through a lot together—in a very short time.

He kissed her cheek, then pressed his face against her hair. "You smell so good," he murmured.

"I was thinking the same thing about you."

"But I'm a guy."

"Good in a very masculine way."

His hands stroked up and down her back. She

was aware of his bare legs below the shirt. Well, more than his bare legs. He was aroused. Yet he didn't pull her against his body.

"So, what do you want to do here?" he asked, his voice low and thick.

"Not as much as you do."

"I just want to be close to you."

She cleared her throat. "Your body says that's a lie."

"Physiological reaction."

"Yeah, sure."

She settled her head against his shoulder, thinking that she might just sleep beside him, warm and safe in his arms.

But as he quietly nuzzled his lips in her hair, stroked her neck and shoulders, she found herself wanting more. Unable to tell him in words, she nibbled her lips against his jaw, feeling the stubble of his beard.

"Maybe I should shave."

"Don't get out of bed."

"Okay." He turned his head, and their lips met in a light, sweet kiss.

He made no demands on her. She was the one who deepened the kiss, opening her mouth, probing his lips with her tongue.

He groaned, gathering her closer. As he had before, he stroked the sides of her breasts, then glided his hands toward the centers, making a low sound when he brushed over her hardened nipples.

"Oh…! You're going to make me come apart, just by doing that," she gasped, then felt her face flame as she realized what she'd said.

"That's quite a compliment," he murmured.

"Don't get a swelled…head."

He laughed, and she liked the sound. His laugh was low and sexy. And very, very warm.

His hand moved to her middle, stroking over the curve of her abdomen.

"I'm fat," she murmured. "And my breasts are so big."

He chuckled. "You're kidding, right? What guy would complain about big breasts?"

"I guess you have a point there," she conceded.

"Don't you know how sexy and feminine you feel to me?" he asked.

"I'm embarrassed by the way I look."

"It's dark in here. I can't see a thing." He reached under the hem of her dress, pushing it slowly up, giving her time to object. She felt herself tense.

He stroked his lips against her jaw and cheek and eyelids as his hand gently explored her body.

"You are lovely."

"But you can't see me."

"Lovely to touch. Smooth skin. Sexy curves."

Rolling her onto her side, he unhooked her bra, then lay down behind her, pressed tight against her. She could feel his almost naked body and his erection wedged against her bottom as he pushed her bra out of the way, then took one breast in his hand, making her cry out again as he teased her nipple.

"Oh, Riley."

One hand moved down her body again and into her panties. She was swollen and wet, and ready for his touch.

Her breath came in little gasps as he stroked her most-sensitive flesh with one hand, while he moved the other from one breast to the other— triggering a shattering orgasm that brought a cry of joy to her lips.

She collapsed back against him, still breathing hard.

"Nice," he whispered, kissing her cheek. "That was so nice."

"And you're still hard as a fence post," she managed to say between panting breaths.

"I'm okay."

Ignoring his quick rejoinder, she said, "I'd like to do something about that."

He breathed in a draft of air and let it out. "What? I mean, you need to tell me what's okay for us to do."

"I think we could. I mean…" She fumbled for the right words, glad that her face was hidden from him. "I think we could make love…with you still in back of me like this. If that would work for you."

"Oh, yeah. It would work just fine for me."

He pushed her panties down, caressing her bottom, and she used her feet and legs to get rid of the flimsy garment. She expected to feel him inside her in the next moment. But he stayed where he was, pressed tightly against her, reaching around to stroke her breasts and her sex again, stoking her pleasure until she was squirming in his arms.

"Riley…please…I need…"

"Yes…."

He angled his hips and slipped inside her from the back, exclaiming in pleasure as she closed tightly around him.

He kept his hands where they had been before, stroking her breasts and between her legs, fueling her pleasure as he moved inside her with measured strokes.

She heard him cry out as his body tensed with release, then she followed him over the edge.

For long moments they lay quietly in the darkened bedroom.

"Was that okay for you?" she finally asked.

He turned her in his arms, kissed her on the mouth. "A lot more than okay."

She wanted to ask what making love had meant to him. And she wanted to ask him if he was ready to tell her what he was really doing at the Golden Saddle Ranch. But she was afraid to speak the words, because she didn't want to hear that he wasn't going to tell her. And she wanted to cherish this time with him. So she settled down beside him and closed her eyes.

She felt him relax, as though he'd been waiting for another question and she'd let him off the hook.

RILEY LAY IN THE DOUBLE BED, holding Courtney while she slept. It was easy to picture himself staying at the Golden Saddle, taking over more than the duties of ranch manager. But he still wasn't free to tell her what he was really doing in her employ. And he knew she was going to hate him when she found out the size of the lies he'd spun her.

It had been a mistake to sleep with her. He should never have invited her into his bed, because the intimacy was only going to make things worse when the final showdown came.

But he had been so needy when she walked into the room that he'd talked her under the covers.

He was the chameleon, the man who could make himself into anyone he wanted. And he'd worked his sleight of hand on Courtney. Maybe he'd even used it on himself this time, because making love with her had felt so damn good. So damn right.

And now he'd better remember who he really was and why he was here. He had a job to do for Big Sky.

He eased away from her and quickly pulled on the pants and boots he'd discarded. He went out to check on Buttercup. And while he was outside in the cold, he tried to figure out how to get his relationship with Courtney back where it belonged.

MAYBE COURTNEY was feeling the same way. He didn't talk to her over the next couple of days, although he did see her near the house a few times.

But he received a communication of another sort. A note from Boone Fowler appeared in the mailbox, and Kelly brought it up with the rest of the mail.

"Crown Prince Nikolai is speaking in Billings tomorrow. I'd like you to attend—so you can really understand what's wrong with this country, where we make a hero of a foreign interloper who's gotten us involved in a war we have no business fighting."

Riley grimaced. Fowler hadn't given him much notice. But at least the meeting was at 7:00 p.m. So he could leave the ranch without shirking his duties.

When he told Kelly he'd be out for the evening, the other man gave him a considering look.

"You're not planning to get drunk, are you?"

Riley shook his head. "I learned my lesson a few days ago. As a matter of fact, I'm going to a lecture."

"Get out of here."

"Crown Prince Nikolai is speaking in Billings. I want to hear him. You want to come along?"

As he'd anticipated, Kelly shook his head.

THE CROWN PRINCE of Lukinburg stood in front of his closet full of expensive suits. He had special luggage for packing his outfits, so they traveled perfectly. And a valet named Boris whose only job was taking care of the prince's clothing.

So what should he wear for the upcoming speech in Billings?

He sniffed derisively. The town fathers had dubbed this one-horse town "The Magic City." He'd been driven around the place in his private limousine. And he was definitely underwhelmed. Billings was a cow town with too much Western flavor. One of the big attractions they bragged about—the Buffalo Bill Historic Center—wasn't even in the same state. And they made a big deal of the Little Big Horn National Monument, where a bunch of Plains Indians wiped out an entire battalion of the Seventh Cavalry.

He laughed. Apparently these Americans were easy to impress. Which was why his choice of clothing was important. All his suits were custom-made by a tailor in London. They all coordinated with shirts and ties from an exclusive Paris house. He fingered a gray silk-and-wool jacket. Then moved on to a blue cashmere blazer. Perhaps a blazer was too casual for the event. Or perhaps the people in Montana would appreciate seeing royalty dressed down a bit for the occasion.

Yes. The blue blazer. And light gray slacks. With a white shirt and a red tie with small blue figures. The colors of the American flag. That would do nicely. The ladies would like the effect. He never forgot about his attraction for the ladies.

Finished with the clothing selection, he turned back to his notes. He had a lot of stock paragraphs. But the wording always had to be changed. And he hadn't gotten tonight's speech exactly right yet. He had to be precise in his delivery—while maintaining rapport with the audience.

Sitting at the desk, he poured himself a drink of

the single-malt scotch he'd come to enjoy. It was a pleasure he could only indulge in private, however. In public he must come across as sober and reliable—a signal to the American public that they could put their faith in him for the future of Lukinburg.

As he sipped the amber liquor, he went over the sheets he'd printed that morning. Skimming over the first part, he got to the words, "And now we begin."

That phrase had a special meaning for his followers in the United States. It was a signal for them to pay close attention to what came next.

He smiled to himself, appreciating his rhetorical skills. He was walking a fine line with this talk, but he was sure it would accomplish exactly what he wanted.

RILEY WALKED into the large VFW hall that the prince had rented. Probably for symbolic reasons. The place was packed—with females making up more than fifty percent of the audience.

He spotted several of Boone Fowler's men in the audience, but not the head honcho himself. Probably they'd been assigned to check up on the new recruit, and he was thankful he'd arrived early enough to get in.

A hush fell on the audience when the mayor

came out to introduce the main attraction. He recited the prince's patriotic credentials, then explained why he was taking his case to the American people.

When Nikolai himself walked onto the stage, he immediately took command of the hall.

Riley had studied pictures of the heir to the Lukinburg throne. But he wasn't prepared for the impression the thirtysomething prince made.

The man stood very still, allowing the thunderous applause to wash over him for several minutes. Riley took in his curly dark hair, dazzlingly white smile, chiseled cheekbones and powerfully elegant physique covered by an expensive sports jacket and slacks. Really, he looked more like a movie star than anything else.

But he carried himself with an air of authority that must have been drummed into him since childhood. When he began to speak, there was absolute silence in the hall.

He described his father's repressive regime, telling the crowd that young girls in his country were forced into marriage, and boys were forced into the army. He proclaimed his opposition to a government that could drain the money from the treasury to build palaces for the king. And he thanked the American people for coming to the aid of his country.

Every few moments, the crowd interrupted him with applause. And when he finished, reporters mobbed the stage, shouting questions.

Riley took notes, in case Fowler was going to quiz him later. He stayed to watch some of the media circus, then drove back to the ranch.

The light was on in the main house when he came up the driveway, and he longed to knock on Courtney's door. To be honest, he longed to crawl under the covers with her again and make love. Maybe this time she'd let him keep the light on while he stroked and kissed those full, firm breasts. Pregnancy had transformed her into a fertility goddess.

He made a low sound as he cut off the fantasy. If he didn't stop thinking about her that way, he was going to explode.

A movement in one of the lighted windows made him glance up. He saw her looking out at him.

More than ever he ached to go to her. Instead he turned toward the bunkhouse, because that was his only honorable option.

HE WAS IN THE BARN early the next morning when Courtney came in. She gave him a long look. When he didn't speak, she cleared her throat.

"You went to hear Prince Nikolai last night?"

"Yeah. Who told you—Kelly?"

"No. Jake." She looked around and spotted the man himself approaching the barn. "Why don't you come up to the house for a cup of tea?"

He might have declined. But he found he couldn't turn down the direct request. "Okay."

They walked in silence to the house. When they were inside with the door closed, she turned to him. "I wasn't expecting you to make any kind of commitment the other night, if that's what you're worried about."

He scuffed his booted foot against the hall floor. "I'm not free to."

"And I get the feeling you're not going to tell me why."

He clenched his fists at his sides, struggling with frustration. "I can't."

She hung up her coat and marched down the hall to the kitchen. He slammed his own coat onto the rack and hurried to follow her.

She was standing at the sink, her shoulders hunched, her head bowed.

He ached to reach for her, but he was afraid that if he did, they'd end up in the bedroom again.

"I need to straighten some things out in my personal life," he said, giving her the only explanation for his behavior that he could. He hadn't been authorized by Big Sky to tell her what was really

going on, and his training was too ingrained to jeop-
ardize the mission for his personal feelings—or
hers.

"And then what?"

"Then we can talk…about us. Don't ask me to
say anything more right now."

She looked as if she wanted to do just that. Instead she ran water into the kettle and set it on the
stove.

"Do you object to my going to see the prince
last night?" he asked.

"No. But I was surprised."

"What do you think of him?" he asked.

"He's charming. And intelligent. As a matter of
fact, I listened to the speech on the radio."

"And?"

"He was educated at Harvard, but he makes
some odd grammatical mistakes. Like using *me*
when he should have said *I*. Or using the wrong
word—or one that's not quite right."

She filled mugs and added the same teabags she
had before.

"Yeah. But basically, he came across pretty
well. Especially to the ladies."

She nodded. "He's so charismatic."

"But you don't agree with his logic."

"Like I told you, I was for the war. Until my…"
She stopped and started over. "My ex-husband

was killed over there. Then I started thinking about all the men we've lost and whether the sacrifice is worth it."

He added sugar to his tea and sipped. "How do most people around here feel?"

"I'm kind of out of touch with most people."

"Mmm."

"But I'm going to the opening of the battered-women's shelter next week."

He sat up straighter. "That doesn't exactly fit in with your policy of staying home where you're safe."

She set her mug down with a thunk. "I won't be a prisoner here. And I think I'll be safe in a crowd."

"Not necessarily."

She ran her finger around the top of the mug, then finally said, "I have to prove this town can't defeat me."

"What's that supposed to mean?"

"I think it's pretty self-explanatory. I can't hide at the ranch forever."

She looked as though she wanted to say something else, and he waited tensely. Apparently she changed her mind, and he left a few minutes later because he didn't want her to see the worry written on his face.

But he stuck close to the ranch yard and kept tabs on her. And when she walked purposefully toward him in the barn the next day, he felt his chest tighten.

"I, uh, wonder if you'd mind going into town with me."

"Why?"

"I need some groceries."

"Can't someone else get them?"

"The person around here who knows how to save money at the grocery store is me."

He gritted his teeth, then made an effort to relax his jaw. "Then I'll certainly come along."

"You don't sound too enthusiastic."

"You know my position on your leaving the ranch."

They glared at each other.

"I can ask someone else."

"I'd rather it be me. Let me tell the hands."

After informing Jake where he was going, he climbed into the cab beside her.

There were a lot of things he wanted to say to her. What came out of his mouth was, "Glad we aren't expecting snow again."

She gave him a sidewise look. "Right."

He wondered if he could think of a dumber comment. After a moment he asked, "So has anything suspicious happened in the house?"

"No," she said quietly, but he'd learned to read her pretty well.

"I don't think you're telling me the truth."

She huffed out a breath. "Okay. It has nothing to do with the house. Somebody followed me from town the other day."

"You mean when you came to get me out of jail," he asked carefully.

"Yes, then."

"And you're just mentioning it."

"I gave him the slip at the big rocks."

If he'd been driving, he would have turned around and headed back to the ranch. Instead, he concentrated on not shouting at her. "I told you to be careful," he said in a deceptively quiet voice.

"I am."

"Like going to town now?"

"I asked you to come with me."

"What about going to the opening of the battered-women's shelter?"

"That's with a big crowd," she said, giving him the line she'd used before.

"Yeah, I've been wondering about their advertising it so widely. Shouldn't they be keeping the location secret—so if a woman comes there, her lowlife husband can't find her."

"Maybe they can operate that way in the city," Courtney answered. "But out here, when you build a new building, everybody knows what it's for."

Riley nodded.

"So they might as well have a grand opening."

"With a lot of people. So somebody could get close to you and stab you in the abdomen, and nobody would see who it was."

She gasped. "Stop it! You're trying to scare me."

"Right."

She gave him a dark look and switched on the radio—loud. He wanted to tell her she was the most obstinate woman he'd ever met. But he knew that his own mother had some of the same qualities. She'd once knifed a man who had followed her to her car and tried to assault her in the parking lot.

Instead of continuing the argument, he settled for watching the scenery.

As they pulled into the grocery store parking lot, which was relatively empty, he scanned the area, looking for trouble—and found it.

The militia was in town. "Oh, great," he muttered.

"What?"

"Fowler and his gang. Go in and pick up some stuff, then let's get out of here."

"I thought you were best buddies with Fowler."

"I never said that."

"What is your relationship with him?"

It was on the tip of his tongue to blurt out the

truth, but he knew it was against regulations, so he kept quiet.

Her head whipped toward him. "Don't ignore me!"

"This conversation is pointless. Go in and get your groceries."

She slammed into a parking space. And he sat in the truck, watching Fowler and his men—unable to banish a tight feeling in his chest.

One of the men had detached himself from the group. It was the guy named Anderson, who had questioned Fowler in the bar.

As Riley watched, he slipped furtively around the back of a row of stores.

Something was going on. But what?

Fowler spotted Riley and waved.

Riley waved back.

The militia leader spoke to the men with him. They walked toward the bar, while Fowler started toward the drugstore farther along the street.

Riley saw Anderson stick his head around the corner, his eyes narrowed. Now what?

Just then he spotted Courtney through the big window at the front of the grocery store. She was pushing her cart toward the door.

Getting out of the truck, he trotted toward the store, arriving just as Courtney stepped into the sunlight.

"Get back inside," he said gruffly.

She froze in place, giving him a shocked look.

He pushed her behind him, just as the shooting started.

Chapter Twelve

Riley shielded Courtney with his body, silently thanking God that she'd asked him to come to town with her. Lord, what if she'd stepped into the line of fire?

He heard the fear in his voice as he growled, "Get back inside. Then get down. Tell everybody in there to get on the damn floor."

"What about you?"

"Get inside!" he said again.

For once in her life, she did as he asked, scrambling away as he crouched low, sheltering himself against the building.

He could see Fowler taking cover behind a parked car. When he looked the other way, he caught a flash of movement and knew that Anderson had ducked back around the corner, gun in hand.

Most of the militia men had said yes every time Fowler said jump.

But this one had dared to talk back in the bar. Now he was making a more direct challenge to his leader's authority. And endangering everyone who happened to be on the streets in Spur City.

So where was Sheriff Pennington when they needed him? Riley snorted. Probably hiding under hisdamn desk.

Riley looked up, seeing Fowler staring at him. In the Special Forces they'd sometimes used hand signals. But he couldn't count on Fowler's knowing any of them. So Riley pointed to himself— then to his right and made a circular motion, indicating that he was going to try and circle around the shooter.

Fowler gave him a small nod.

Moving quickly, Riley drew his gun and sprinted around the back of the grocery. He was moving fast, looking for Anderson.

He paused behind a Dumpster, his breath coming hard. No sign of the would-be assassin. So which way had the guy gone?

Riley moved cautiously, step by step, looking in doorways and behind heaps of trash.

Finally he spotted the gunman crouched down behind a storage shed, waiting for Fowler to walk into his line of vision.

Riley picked up a tin can and tossed it against the wall of a nearby building.

Anderson whirled and fired at the spot where the can had landed.

Then another shot rang out—then another as Anderson keeled over.

Fowler stepped from the corner of the building, gun in hand. "Got ya," he growled as he went down beside his former comrade in arms to make sure he was dead.

With a satisfied look, he lifted his head toward Riley. "Good work."

"Thanks," he answered, still coping with the cold-blooded execution. Fowler hadn't been in immediate danger. But he'd simply pulled out his gun and shot.

"You drew his attention, so I could get him. But we'll say he had his gun pointed at me."

Before he could answer, running footsteps had them both looking up. Pennington had finally put in his appearance, followed by several of the militia.

"Boone, what happened?" the sheriff puffed.

"It looks like Anderson had a brain snap. He tried to kill me, and I shot him in self-defense." Fowler raised his head. "Riley here saw it all. He can back me up."

"Yeah," Riley answered, almost gagging on the lie.

"What were you doing here?" Pennington asked.

"I came into town to take Ms. Rogers to the grocery store. She was coming out when the shooting started. I circled around to get the guy's attention. But he spotted Boone first."

Pennington turned back to Fowler. "Why'd he go after you?"

"He wanted to take my place in the organization."

The sheriff whistled through his teeth.

Other people had begun to come from wherever they'd hidden when the shooting started.

"I don't want any trouble," Fowler said in a low voice.

Pennington gave him a small nod, then spoke for the benefit of the crowd. "You two need to come down to the office to make a statement. And I need to call the coroner's office." He pulled his cell phone from his pocket and punched in a number.

Riley still couldn't believe how Fowler had managed to get Pennington in his pocket. Either he had something big he was blackmailing the sheriff with, or the lawman was just too cowardly to cross him. Either way, there was no doubt who was really runningthis town.

Riley turned to Fowler. "I'd better make sure Ms. Rogers is okay."

"What…! You're all concerned about her?"

"I want to keep my job. Tell Pennington I'll meet you at the office."

Before the sheriff could object, he turned and hurried back to the grocery store, where he found a crowd of worried people gathered near the door. Courtney was among them.

"I thought I told you to stay inside," Riley clipped out.

At the sound of his voice, relief suffused her features. "Riley, thank the Lord."

She rushed to him, then stopped, apparently mindful that a bunch of bystanders was now staring at them.

He wanted to clasp her tightly in his arms. She looked like she had the same thing in mind. But they merely stood facing each other, arms at their sides.

He glanced around at the anxious faces. "Apparently one of Fowler's guys…wigged out," he said. "He's dead now."

"There was a lot of shooting," somebody called out. "What happened?"

Riley addressed the onlooker. "Fowler nailed him. Sheriff Pennington is taking care of things."

Someone snickered. "Oh, yeah. Now that the shooting's stopped."

Apparently the citizens of Spur City had a pretty low opinion of the lawman.

Some people hurried off in the direction from which Riley had come. He didn't stop them. Let the sheriff take care of crowd control.

Murmurs came from the bystanders. Riley turned back to Courtney and lowered his voice. "Are you okay?"

"Yes. Are you?"

He nodded. "But I've got to go give a statement to the sheriff—since I was there when it happened. Really, I shouldn't have left the scene. But I wanted to make sure you were okay. I don't know how long I'm going to be. You'd better go on home."

She gave him a doubtful look. "What about you?"

"I'll catch a ride."

"With whom?" she said, her voice turning sharp. And he was pretty sure she was picturing him cozying up to Fowler.

He was thinking the same thing. Anderson had handed him a golden opportunity. But he wasn't going to share that observation with Courtney.

He turned his hands palm up. "I can't stand here talking. I have to get back there before Pennington comes looking for me."

With that excuse, he turned and strode back to the shooting scene.

The sheriff looked up as he returned. "Nice of you to join us."

"I had business to take care of."

When a deputy arrived, he ushered them to the sheriff's office, where Riley and Fowler both wrote out what had happened. Riley knew that they should have been put in separate rooms. But Fowler sat at the sheriff's desk, and Riley sat in one of his guest chairs—using a stack of gun magazines as a writing surface, spewing out the scenario Fowler had suggested. A couple of times, the militia leader asked him questions before he wrote. And two of his men came in to make comments, adding details he could use.

After Pennington came in and read the statements, he told them they could go.

"You said you drove to town with Ms. Rogers," Fowler said. "You need a ride home?"

"Yeah."

"That will give us a chance to talk."

Riley nodded as he followed Fowler to an SUV parked down the street. The inside reeked of cigarette smoke, and the ashtray overflowed. Fowler emptied it beside the car door before they pulled away and headed in the direction of the ranch.

"You're a good man to have in a fight," he said to Riley.

"I try."

"Army training?"

"Yeah."

"Me, too." He laughed. "The good old U.S. Army taught me everything I know."

Riley joined in the laughter, hoping he sounded as jolly as the militia leader.

"Anderson started off okay," Fowler went on. "But he overestimated his own importance. Then he started challenging me. You heard him the other day at the bar."

"Mmm-hmm."

"Before we got you out of jail, he told me you were a hothead." Fowler laughed. "He was the hothead."

"Apparently," Riley agreed.

"So how would you like to be my second in command?" Fowler asked.

"I'm flattered, of course."

"Think about it seriously." Fowler cleared his throat. "How did you like the prince's speech?"

"He's a good speaker. I didn't much like his message."

"You can say that again. We've got a plan to fix his wagon."

"What?"

"You know how our troops just carried out a surgical strike in Lukinburg? To get some of the top guys in their government."

"I don't keep up with the news."

"You should."

"There's only one television set in the bunk-house. And we don't get the paper out at the ranch."

"You need to keep informed."

"What's your point about the attack in Lukinburg?" Riley asked.

Fowler took his eyes off the road for a moment. "We're going to do the same thing here."

Riley whistled through his teeth. "We? As in you and your men?"

"Yup."

"And how are you going to pull that off?"

"You know that battered-women's shelter that they're opening in town tomorrow night?"

Riley nodded. "Uh-huh."

"We're going to attack it." He grinned. "We'll kill a bunch of local officials. But better than that— we're going to get the first lady of the United States."

Riley felt like he'd been sucker punched in the gut. He didn't have to fake astonishment when he said, "Whoa! You'd better explain that."

"It's one of her good works. She's a sponsor of the shelter. And she's coming to the grand opening. That's supposed to be a big freaking secret. But of course Pennington knows about it, and he told us."

Riley managed to say, "How are you going to pull off the attack?"

"We've got advance information."

"From whom?"

"I'll just keep that to myself for the time being. The important point is that we sneak up on the place and let them have it."

"Like how exactly?"

"I never give out my plans until we're ready to go."

"Smart," Riley answered, inwardly cursing. "You've got a devious mind."

"Thanks. You're with us, right?"

"Of course."

"I was counting on you."

"How many guys are you bringing?" Riley asked.

"All fifteen of us. Just to make sure it goes off as planned."

"Good."

"The shelter is in an isolated location. So we can hide out in the woods."

"Won't the Secret Service be there?"

"Yeah. But so what? They won't be expecting anything funny in a backwater Montana town. And they don't know how to handle themselves out here in the wilderness."

"True." He kept his voice even, but he was thinking he had to get this information to Big Sky immediately. "So what do you want me to do?" he asked.

"I'll determine that. But you see why I can't let you go back to the ranch?"

At the casually spoken words, Riley's gut clenched. "Yeah. I see," he said carefully. He'd just found out a great deal of mind-blowing information, and he had no idea how he was going to tell Big Sky—or Courtney Rogers, for that matter.

"You'll stay with us until tomorrow. Then we'll all leave together."

"So you don't trust me?"

"I want to. But I have to be careful, you know."

"Understood."

They had reached the entrance to the ranch, and Fowler drove past—then took the lane he'd drawn on the map several days earlier.

Riley sat next to him, feeling sick, wondering what the hell he was going to do now.

FOWLER HEADED UP A ROAD that was even worse than the main entrance to the ranch.

"I left my stuff in the bunkhouse," Riley said.

"We can buy you new things after this operation. For now we've got standard-issue fatigues. You can borrow a uniform."

"And a gun?" Riley inquired.

"You'll be issued a sidearm—when we leave for the women's shelter."

"Okay."

Fowler pulled up in front of a collection of weathered buildings that Courtney had said her father had built as a camp.

"A little primitive," Fowler said as he watched Riley eyeing the militia headquarters. "But I'm expecting to move to more upscale digs soon."

"How come?"

"We've got a line on better financing."

As Fowler pulled up, several men dressed in army fatigues came out of the building and eyed Riley. They didn't look surprised, and he figured that the guys who had come to town with Fowler had already reported the big news.

The men gathered around, and the militia leader told how Anderson had tried to kill him—and Riley had risked his life in the gun battle.

Establishing his credentials as a tough guy was a great introduction to the group.

He met the gang, some of whom he had already encountered at the bar the other morning. Tipton and Drake and Walters stood out in his mind as being particularly ruthless.

And he wasn't all that surprised to meet a guy with a scar on his face—a man named Nichols. Courtney's former ranch hand. As Riley had suspected, the scumbag had joined the bad guys.

Riley struggled to act natural, when his mind

was desperately scrambling for a way to get a message to Big Sky.

That wouldn't be anytime soon, because it was obvious the men were watching him. And even though Fowler was acting friendly, Riley knew he didn't totally trust his new recruit.

COURTNEY LOOKED DOWN the road, watching and waiting for Riley. It was getting dark now, and she had been expecting him long ago.

How much time could it take to write out a report of the shooting?

She didn't know. But five hours seemed excessive.

So where was he now? She paced back and forth in front of the window, then put on her coat and went outside.

Maybe he was in trouble. Maybe Pennington had made up some charge and put Riley in jail. Could he be the one charged with the killing?

She clenched her gloved hands into fists, worry and anger warring inside of her.

What if he'd gone off somewhere to have a couple of drinks with Fowler? What if he'd gotten drunk again? Maybe that was the reason Pennington was holding him. Only this time it would be worse, because it was his second offense in town.

"Stop it," she ordered herself. "You're making things up. He's not in jail. He'll be back soon."

Billy crossed the ranch yard and stopped a few yards from her. "Go in and have a cup of tea. I'll let you know when Riley comes home."

Apparently her worry was obvious. She nodded and went back into the house. But she didn't want the tea. Instead she turned off the living room light and opened the blinds so she could stare out into the night, looking for headlights.

In the darkened room, she dozed off.

Then a knock at the door made her jump. Scrambling out of her chair, she swayed on unsteady legs and had to reach out a hand to catch herself.

The knock sounded again, this time more insistent.

"I'll be right there," she called out.

When she felt more stable, she hurried across the room and into the hall, where she switched on the light and threw open the door, ready to hurl sharp words at Riley for making her worry about him.

But she found Jake standing on the porch, a smug expression on his lined face.

"What?" she demanded, stepping aside so he could come in out of the cold. From the way he looked, she was pretty sure she wasn't going to like what he had to say.

He closed the door behind him, then turned to face her. "I went into town," he said. "To look for Watson."

"And?"

"And he left with that Boone Fowler guy."

"Get to the point," she snapped.

"I asked around. A couple of the lowlife militia guys came into town later. They say Watson joined them."

"You mean they're not environmentalists?"

"Afraid not."

Chapter Thirteen

Courtney caught her breath. "Riley Watson is out at the militia camp?" she asked, hardly able to wrap her mind around the concept.

"And he's going to stay with those guys," Jake added. "Or…that's the way they tell it."

Courtney struggled to catch her breath. Feeling dizzy, she steadied herself against the wall.

Jake folded his lips over his teeth. "I'm sorry to bring you the bad news."

"No you're not. You're happy about it," Courtney retorted.

Jake shifted his weight from one foot to the other. "I never liked the guy. I'm glad you're rid of him."

"I…" She was about to say she needed Riley. But she stopped herself before she said anything she was going to regret.

"Thank you for telling me," she managed.

"What do you want me to do with his stuff?"

"Leave it where it is. If he wants it, he can come back for it," Courtney whispered, knowing that if she spoke louder she might start to cry.

"I'll go on now." Mercifully, Jake turned and left her alone before she made a fool of herself.

She said nothing, only watched him leave. As he closed the door, tears slipped down her cheeks.

She had entertained fantasies about Riley Watson. And she had made love with him. She would never have done that if she hadn't cared about him, but he'd crawled under her defenses all too easily. Well, that just went to prove that she was wonderful at picking the wrong men.

Making herself vulnerable to Riley had been a big mistake. She'd been a fool to think that anything could come of that. And a fool to trust him.

The moment he got a better offer, he had bailed out. Probably he was out at Fowler's compound telling stories about how he'd gotten into her pants.

So she'd better stop making up fairy stories about how he was going to stay here and help her raise her daughter.

BOONE FOWLER HIMSELF showed Riley around the militia compound, pointing out the high points of his domain with pride.

Riley hoped he sounded impressed—and interested in this two-bit operation—when his insides were jumping like a bullfrog on a hot griddle.

He was pretty sure Courtney was worried about him. Or mad as hell that he hadn't come back to the ranch. Knowing he'd hurt her made him sick. But he had no other option. His assignment was to get in solid with the militia leader, and he'd done that.

So he played eager new recruit, making noises about Fowler's impressive arsenal and the state of readiness of his troops while he watched for a chance to be alone.

As he toured the compound, he saw that the living arrangements vastly complicated his problem. There was no privacy.

Fowler showed him to a dingy bedroom that he'd have to share with three other guys. And he saw that all the troops ate in a communal mess hall.

He knew he'd get caught if he tried to sneak away at night. So what the hell was he going to do?

He got a lucky break after weapons training and before dinner in the mess hall.

"So where's the men's room?" he asked the guy named Walters. "I haven't seen a pot to piss in. Are we supposed to go in the woods?"

"We got an outhouse out back. And there's a couple of cold water faucets in the wash shed."

Riley's nose wrinkled. "Pretty primitive."

"It builds character. You get used to it," Walters said.

Riley repaired to the outside toilet facility and closed the door. The moment he was alone, he called Big Sky.

The colonel answered the phone immediately. "I hear there was a shooting in Spur City."

"I don't have time for chitchat. One of Fowler's men started shooting at him. And I saved the head honcho's life. He took me back to the compound with him. I'm talking from the only place where I can get any privacy. The outhouse."

The colonel snickered.

"I wish it were funny." He gave Murphy a quick summary of what was going down at the battered-women's shelter—including the information that the first lady of the United States was the surprise guest of honor.

The colonel whistled through his teeth.

"Be there," Riley gave his commander an order.

"We will."

"One more thing—Fowler is getting backing from someone with money."

"Did he confirm that it's King Aleksandr Petrov…or anyone else?"

"No. He's staying tight-lipped about the person's identity. You're keeping tabs on him. Have you seen him with anyone in town who could give us a lead?"

"No."

Someone banged on the outhouse door. "You fall in or something?"

Riley hung up abruptly, hoping to hell that Big Sky had enough time to get into position at the shelter before the bad guys arrived.

Riley spent the rest of the evening and the next day trading war stories with Fowler and his troops and trying to pretend he fit in—when all the time he felt his flesh crawling. But now he saw they were watching him more closely. Somebody was with him at all times—even waiting outside the outhouse for him, which meant he couldn't call Courtney the way he'd called Big Sky.

THE MORNING of the big opening dawned bright and crisp. A beautiful day, Riley thought as he ate baked beans and franks for breakfast and drank rot-gut coffee, along with the rest of the troops.

Fowler had a planning session later in the morning, where he put up a diagram of the battered-women's shelter and the nearby national park, and used a pointer to show everyone where they'd be located. Then he had them practice the actual raid—with some of the gang playing themselves and some playing Secret Service dudes, as Fowler called them.

The whole exercise turned Riley's stomach, but it helped pass the endless hours until they would leave for the night's assignment.

He kept thinking about the people these bozos were planning to attack. Courtney was supposed to be there. And he wanted to warn her. But he couldn't make any more phone calls.

As evening approached, the sense of doom increased. Big Sky hadn't had much time to prepare. What the hell were they going to do to save innocent lives?

He'd given up on warning Courtney. All he could do was pray that he could keep her out of the line of fire—the way he'd done yesterday.

Just before they left, Fowler called him aside.

"You think Ms. Rogers is coming to the opening?" he asked.

"Don't know," Riley answered.

"Well, if she did, that would kill two birds with one stone."

"What do you mean?" Riley asked, struggling to keep his tone even.

"She's a pain in the ass. I mean, once I get rid of her, I can run her ranch better than she does."

"You sure could," Riley said, hoping he didn't sound like he wanted to kill the man.

"I had one of the guys take a shot at her. He almost got her that time, but it was snowing, and he missed. Then another time, he tried to follow her from town. But she slipped away again."

"Which guy?"

Fowler's eyes narrowed dangerously. "Why do you care?"

"Just curious."

"Drake. And I had Nichols going over to her place at night to pick up information. He used to work for her, and he didn't like her much."

"She can be hard to take," Riley managed.

"We also booby trapped an old cabin out there. I heard it blow up."

Riley nodded tightly.

Fowler gave him a piercing look. "What?"

"I think I almost got killed in some of your booby traps. You had a pit dug, too. Didn't you?"

"Yeah."

"I wish I'd had a clue."

"Sorry. If I'd known it was you, I would have—" he shrugged.

"Water under the bridge," Riley answered, keeping his hands hanging at his sides when he wanted to wrap them around the guy's throat.

Fowler waved an arm, dismissing the subject, then took up another. "To make up for the insult, I got a choice assignment for you."

"Sure."

"I want you to drive one of the getaway vehicles," he said.

"Okay," Riley answered, hoping he didn't look as if he thought Fowler had just handed him a big Christmas present.

"Drake will go with you."

"I'm glad to have the company," he answered, wondering how he could sit next to the man without shooting him. And wondering how he was going to get rid of the bastard. He'd thought Fowler was giving him a break. It turned out to have strings attached.

They started out for the battered-women's center just after dark, with Riley holding back and getting into position at the rear of the column.

As they approached the turnoff to the ranch, he slowed down.

"Boone told me about your taking a shot at Mrs. Rogers."

"Yeah. That was fun. Too bad I missed."

Riley gritted his teeth to keep from cursing, then slowed the vehicle some more.

"What?" Drake asked.

"Something's wrong with one of the front tires."

"I don't feel nothin'."

"Well, I do, and I'm going to have a look."

Riley pulled onto the shoulder and got out. Drake waited in the cab.

"Come look at this," Riley called out.

Drake muttered an expletive, but he got out and came around to Riley's side of the vehicle.

When the militia man bent down, Riley moved in behind him.

"Hey, I don't see nothin'."

"It's right here."

Riley hit him over the head with the butt of his gun. "That's for trying to kill Courtney," he muttered as he tied and gagged him with the rope and undershirt he'd brought along.

He turned in at the ranch, speeding up the driveway and pulling to a halt in the ranch yard.

As he jumped out and hurried toward the house, Jake appeared in front of him. Riley stopped short. Once again, Jake was holding a gun.

"Where are you going?" the older man demanded.

"I've got to talk to Courtney."

"No way am I letting you get close to her."

"Jake, I don't have much time."

"Yeah, you've got to get back to those militia friends of yours."

He debated spitting out the truth. But he still didn't know where Jake stood. He could be the spy at the ranch, and no way could Riley take a chance on the whole mission blowing up in the collective faces of Big Sky because of old Jake. This was their best chance to round up the militia leader and his new gang of thugs.

"Ask her if she'll talk to me," he said, using a wheedling tone.

"I'm not going to upset her by telling her you sneaked back on the ranch."

A noise from the truck came to Riley's rescue. Drake must have come to—and was trying to shout around the gag.

"What's that?" Jake demanded, his attention shifting toward the vehicle.

Riley used the distraction to come down in a chopping motion on Jake's gun hand.

Jake made a startled exclamation. For the second time that night, Riley bashed a man's head with the butt of his gun. This time not as hard.

Picking up Jake, he ran with him toward the house.

Courtney must have heard something outside, because she was already at the door—and armed. She was wearing a dress coat and boots. He assumed she was dolled up to attend the shelter's opening ceremonies.

"What in the Sam Hill is going on?" she demanded as she took in the picture the two men made. "What have you done to Jake?"

"He was trying to keep me away from you, and we have to talk."

"We're done talking—and anything else of a personal nature."

He pushed past her, strode into the living room and laid Jake on the couch.

Courtney followed, her eyes angry. "You can't just put him on the sofa and leave."

"Yeah, I can. And you'd better take care of him."

"Damn you," Courtney spat out.

He gave her a direct look. "I came to warn you. Stay away from the opening tonight. The militia are going to make trouble. But don't tell Jake where I'm going."

"What kind of trouble?'

He looked around and lowered his voice. "I can't talk about it. But we've got it under control." He hoped to hell he was telling the truth.

"We who?"

"My...buddies and me."

She wedged her hands on her hips, which thrust her belly toward him. "I've thought for a long time that you're not what you say you are. Do you work for a government agency?"

"No. And I can't stand here jawing. I have to get back before Fowler sees I'm missing—and executes me on the spot."

She winced. "Would he do that?"

"He might." He made his voice hard. "Fowler told me he was the one who ordered the shooting at the bridge. And he had you followed."

She gasped.

"So just do the smart thing tonight. Do us both a big favor and stay home. And don't call the sheriff, because he's one of the bad guys."

"How do you know?"

"By the way he handled the murder investigation. He was deferring to Fowler."

She stared at him, wide-eyed.

He went on quickly, pressing his advantage. "I'm taking a big chance coming here. But I had to warn you." That was the best he could do. He wanted to make sure she kept herself safe. Now he couldn't stay another second. So he turned and raced back to the truck.

Drake was in the back, thrashing around. He stopped moving and gave Riley a fierce, angry look—as if he'd heard everything.

Well, too bad. Riley tightened the gag, then checked his captive's bonds before climbing back into the driver's seat and speeding down the ranch road.

If he could catch up with the convoy before they got to the shelter, he'd be in good shape. If he couldn't, then Fowler might start asking questions.

But what about Drake? Which was more dangerous—taking the man with him or dropping him on his head somewhere?

COURTNEY BENT TOWARD JAKE. He groaned and moved, and she felt the lump on the back of his head.

His eyes fluttered open. Before he even knew where he was, he reached for his gun—which wasn't in its holster, thank the Lord.

"Where is he?" Jake demanded, trying to sit up.

She pressed a hand to his shoulder. "Stay where you are for a few minutes."

"I have to get that bastard."

"He's gone."

"Where?"

Courtney hesitated. If she told Jake Riley's story, he'd probably rush to the women's shelter. And that might throw a monkey wrench into Riley's plans.

But was he even telling the truth? She clenched her teeth. It was obvious he didn't want her to go to the shelter. That he didn't want her to get hurt. Still, that didn't mean he was one of the good guys. He could simply be acting on his feelings for her.

So what was she going to do? Believe what he'd told her…or call the sheriff?

"Where is he?" Jake asked again.

"He's left. He had business to take care of."

"You trust him?"

"I want to."

"You're making a mistake," Jake growled.

"Let me take care of your head."

"I'm fine. You go on to that meeting."

"I'm staying with you," she answered.

His eyes narrowed as he looked at her. "Oh, yeah? Because you're worried about me...or because of something that bastard told you?"

"Both," she admitted in a small voice.

RILEY SPED INTO THE NIGHT. He saw a line of taillights on the road ahead of him and gave silent thanks. Then he caught up with the car at the end of the line and realized he was only seeing traffic on the highway—probably people heading for the shelter opening.

He slowed, looking for the back road into the national park that Fowler had directed them to take. When he saw a narrow lane, he hoped he'd found the right place and turned off.

A vehicle loomed in front of him, blocking his path, and armed men got out.

It was the militia, using the national park like it was their private camping grounds.

Walters strode toward him, gun drawn.

"Don't shoot. It's me," Riley called out.

"Where the hell have you been?"

Riley thought fast. "Drake turned out to be a little skittish about the assignment. He got sick, and I had to stop at the side of the road a couple of times."

Walters laughed. "Yeah, he *was* a mite nervous."

"Then I got caught in traffic."

Walters looked around. "So where is Drake now?"

"The last time I stopped, he took off. I guess he was too yellow to stick around," Riley answered, thanking God that he'd decided to leave the man tied up in a stand of trees beside the road. Someone would have to go back for him later—before he froze to death.

Walters walked toward the truck and looked in the cab, then looked in the back. He seemed satisfied with what he saw.

"I'm going to go and get into position…and you need to do the same," Riley said.

He climbed back into his vehicle, turned around so he was prepared for a quick getaway, then walked up the road to where the other men were hidden.

There was no sign of Big Sky. Where the hell were the bounty hunters?

Fowler gathered the men. Apparently he was finally willing to let them in on his plans. "The meeting is in the cafeteria. They set it up like an auditorium—with a wooden stage at one end. We can go in the back." He gave the men a satisfied look. "The first lady of the United frigging States is in there. So we're hunting big game."

There were exclamations of appreciation from the men.

"How do you know?" one guy asked.

"Inside information," Fowler said proudly.

"That silent partner you told us about?"

"Yeah," Fowler allowed. "And we don't want to let them down. So here's the scoop. We sneak up on the place through the woods. Then we take out the guards at the door. After that, we all go in through the back of the building. I'll take the first lady and the chairman of the committee. Tipton, you drill Mrs. Rogers. The rest of you can aim for anyone you want in the audience. Make it random—so nobody knows who's next. But we don't stay more than a couple of minutes. We're in and out of there." He looked at Riley. "You stay with the vehicles."

"I want to be in on the shooting," Riley said, thinking that if Big Sky hadn't arrived, he was going to have to stop these bastards.

"You do what I tell you," Fowler growled.

"Yes, sir," Riley answered, praying that Courtney had listened to him for once and stayed home. As soon as the militia was inside the building, he'd create a distraction—like some shooting outside.

Would that be enough to warn the people who had come to the opening? Well, they were Western ranchers. They'd take cover if they heard gunfire. And the Secret Service would hustle the first lady out of there. He hoped.

Still, he felt his tension mount as Fowler led the men toward the back of the shelter where two guards covered the door.

Riley's sense of doom grew as two of Fowler's men knocked out the guards. The others rushed across the space between the woods and then to the back of the building.

When they were all assembled, Fowler opened the door, and the militia filed in, with their leader taking up the rear—showing his yellow stripe.

The door closed, and Riley tensed. Before he could start shooting into the air, he heard a tremendous boom—followed by a fireball that blew the door off its hinges and into the frigid night.

Chapter Fourteen

The fireball sent Cameron Murphy and his men—Jacob Powell, Trevor Blackhaw, Bryce Martin and the others—diving for cover.

When the colonel raised his head, he saw that the women's shelter was in flames. As he watched, a man came from behind the building and dashed toward the front door.

It was Riley Watson.

"Watson, wait!"

"Not likely."

Cam cursed. He'd promised Watson that he'd be there to prevent whatever the militia men had in mind. But before they'd reached the women's shelter, he and his men had gotten stopped by the Secret Service.

Big Sky was heavily armed and suspicious looking. They'd been held under armed guard, and no amount of talking about an attack from the militia men had convinced the federal agents that they were playing right into Boone Fowler's hands.

"It looks like you got the wrong guys," Cam snapped to the Secret Service agents guarding them. "Let us help."

The agents didn't bother to apologize. They simply nodded, then took off toward the chaos created by the fire.

"Follow Watson," Cameron shouted. "I'll be there as soon as I call 911."

His men rushed for the windows, using logs from the edge of the parking lot to bash out the panes while he made a frantic call, asking for fire and ambulance assistance. Then he followed his men inside. The fire was at the back, thank God. In the kitchen area. People were stampeding toward the front door. The men from Big Sky helped calm down the crowd so they could be evacuated in an orderly manner.

He saw Secret Service men hustle the first lady through one of the windows. Thankful that she was out of danger, he pressed farther into the building and picked up a woman who had been overcome with smoke.

All the time, he kept his eyes peeled for Riley Watson. But the chameleon had vanished into the smoke and confusion of the fire scene.

Cam cursed again. He'd sent Watson on a dangerous mission—to make contact with Boone

Fowler. Then he'd let him down at the crucial moment. If the man didn't come out of that burning building, it would be his fault.

"Clark, Lombardi, see if you can find Watson," he shouted at two of his bounty hunters as he carried an old lady toward the door.

Dazed victims flooded into the open space in front of the shelter. Snow began to fall, adding to their misery.

To get out of the elements, some people staggered to their cars.

The limousines with the first lady and her Secret Service escort sped away into the night. At least she was safe.

In the distance, sirens wailed. Fire and rescue were finally on their way.

As the men from Big Sky kept up their tireless rescue effort, Cam scanned the crowd for Riley Watson—his heart sinking when the agent failed to appear.

He'd just about given up hope when he finally spotted a man covered with smoke and soot helping an older woman toward one of the ambulances that had arrived. The guy seemed familiar. Cam looked harder.

"Watson?"

A grin spread across the man's grimy face. "None other."

"Thank God. I thought you'd bought the farm."

RILEY DRAGGED IN A DRAFT of the cold night air. To be truthful, he felt winded—as though his lungs weren't functioning quite right. But he ignored the breathless sensation. Tilting his head to one side he wheezed, "It's hard to get rid of me."

"I see that. Thank God you made it."

Riley turned the woman over to the medics. Then he gave his commanding officer a long look. "I was counting on you to get here and scoop up the militia men. What the hell happened?"

The colonel's features hardened. "I guess the Secret Service thought we were terrorists. They had us corralled over to the side."

Riley swore, then lowered his voice when he caught some of the firebomb victims looking at him.

Murphy led him away from the crowd. Blackhaw, Campbell, Mike Clark and a bunch of his comrades joined them.

He'd never been so glad in his life to see their familiar faces. They were all tough guys, but they all embraced him like tsunami victims who had each thought the other was dead.

"The firebomb was set at the back—just where the militia went in," Riley said when he had control of his emotions.

"So either they made a bad mistake…or somebody set them up."

"We've been thinking they were working with the terrorists King Aleksandr hired to influence American public opinion," Campbell said.

"Yeah, but what if the terrorists were just using them—and figured this was a good way of getting rid of a dangerous group of hotheads?" Blackhaw suggested.

"That would make sense," the colonel agreed.

They moved to the burned-out entrance the militia had used.

"From the inside, this end of the building is completely destroyed. I couldn't get back there," Riley said, trying not to gasp as he spoke.

The colonel gave him a long look. "Are you all right?"

"Yeah, fine," he insisted. He might have given up and gone back to the medics, but he knew there were people who needed treatment more than he did.

"It looks like the militia all got trapped in the fire," Clark said.

"We'd better make sure of that," the colonel ordered.

"There's one of them tied up along the highway," Riley said. "A guy named Drake. He's the bastard who shot at Courtney from the bridge."

Murphy gave him a considering look, and he

knew he'd let too much emotion leach into his voice.

In a more matter-of-fact tone, he added, "He's point three miles from the entrance to the Golden Saddle Ranch. Maybe he can give you some information."

The colonel didn't spare the time to ask for explanations. But he sent Cook back to pick up Drake—so he could stand trial for attempted murder.

The remaining men fanned out, looking for survivors. The snow near the building had completely melted, but when Riley reached the trees, he spotted a set of ragged footprints leading away—toward where the getaway vehicles had been parked.

He picked up his pace in time to see a man heading for one of the lead trucks. It looked like Fowler.

Riley reached for his gun and realized he'd lost it while he'd been helping get people out of the building.

Without sparing the breath for a curse, he put on a burst of speed, caught up with the guy and grabbed his arm.

Fowler spun around.

"Hey, man, wait up," Riley tried. "I'll drive."

The militia leader gave him an angry look. "No way, you bastard. I saw you in the middle of the rescue operation."

There was no use arguing the point. Instead of wasting any more breath, Riley hauled off and socked the guy. But Riley was in no shape for a fight. The punch was weak, and he knew that he should have called for backup before starting anything.

Fowler had apparently also lost his gun. Instead, he pulled a knife and slashed at Riley's middle. Putting up an arm, he deflected the blade, but it ripped through his coat and into his flesh.

Fowler might have gone for him again, but a shout warned him that the cavalry was coming. Cutting his losses, he ran to one of the trucks and grabbed an assault rifle. Then he turned and ran into the woods.

Riley tried to struggle to his feet.

Clark knelt beside him. "You're wounded."

"I'm…"

"You're out of the action," his buddy said.

"I let him get away."

"He can't get far. Stay here. I'll be right back."

Too exhausted to protest, Riley closed his eyes. The next thing he knew, a medic was leaning over him.

"He's been cut," Clark said. "And he's suffering from smoke inhalation."

The medic looked at the blood on his coat. "You're coming with us," he announced.

Riley glared at Clark.

"Do what he tells you," his friend said, then went to join the rest of the bounty hunters.

CAMERON MURPHY LED his men into the woods. A kind of sick excitement bubbled up inside him.

Big Sky had been the perfect job for a man with his background. But *this* bounty was gutwrenchingly personal.

Cam had been waiting five years for the chance to make sure Boone Fowler got everything he deserved. The militia leader had killed Cam's sister in a government building bombing. And almost killed his wife, Mia, while they were hunting him down. Now he was finally going to even the score with the bastard.

Fowler had a head start. But Big Sky had the advantage of a dozen eyes and ears. Going into search mode, his men spread out, combing the woods. It seemed like hours before Aidan Campbell called out, "Over here."

Cam and the others rushed to the spot. In the sparse snow under the trees, they could see a single trail of footprints.

He could tell that Fowler wasn't quite steady on his feet. It looked like he was hurt. Good. That would slow him down.

Moving as silently as possible, they followed the militia leader's spoor.

He was making for a rocky area, and Cam muttered a curse when the footsteps momentarily disappeared.

As he paused to consider his next move, a hail of bullets slammed into a nearby tree. Fowler had gone for a surprise attack.

"Down!" he shouted.

Everybody hit the ground, then scuttled for cover.

"You keep him pinned down," Cam ordered. "I'm going to circle around."

"Not alone," Trevor Blackhaw informed him.

He gave his friend a sharp look but didn't argue because he knew that going in by himself was a bad idea. And he wasn't planning to make his wife a widow if he could help it.

Weapons at the ready, he and Blackhaw moved as quietly as they could through the woods, circling around Fowler's position. The militia leader continued to exchange fire with the rest of the men, and Cam figured they were keeping him busy.

Finally, they were in position directly behind their quarry.

He motioned Blackhaw down, then crouched a few yards away.

"In back of you," he shouted.

Fowler whirled, firing as he turned.

Cameron shot him three times, watching with

a kind of dreamlike satisfaction as the bastard toppled backward.

He and Blackhaw sprinted down into the rock depression where Fowler had been holed up. He lay on his back, eyes closed and blood leaking from his mouth.

Squatting, Cameron leaned over him. Fowler's eyes flickered open.

"You're supposed to be dead," the militia leader wheezed.

"Yeah, well, I guess the joke is on you."

Neither of them laughed.

"We didn't get blown up like you thought. And in case you haven't figured it out—Riley Watson is working for me. The last time you saw him his name was Craig O'Riley. He tricked you into thinking he was a different guy. You even invited him to join your organization."

Fowler coughed. "No."

"Afraid so. And I've got some more bad news for you. Your friends, the terrorists from Lukinburg, double-crossed you. That fire was rigged before you arrived at the battered-women's shelter. It was meant to take you out."

Fowler's jaw firmed, but he said nothing.

"But you can get even with whoever set you up— by giving me his name," Cam suggested. "You can screw up his communications if you tell me how he contacted you."

Fowler's lips moved.

Cameron leaned closer, ready to hear the information he'd been seeking for months.

"See you in hell," Fowler spat, then went still.

And Cam was left staring into a dead man's face. Thanks to Riley Watson's excellent advance work, he'd finally evened the score. But it felt like a hollow victory.

RILEY WAS FIGHTING with the doctors when Cameron Murphy and Bryce Martin showed up at the hospital.

"If this guy is giving you a hard time, we can take him off your hands," the colonel said.

The physician looked relieved. "Keep him quiet for the next twenty-four hours, if you can."

"Will do."

"What happened?" Riley demanded.

The colonel filled him in on Fowler's demise. "Now we just have to figure out who was backing him."

"And how he was getting his orders."

Murphy nodded. "Yeah, I'd like to know that." He gave Riley a direct look. "Do you mind staying at the ranch for a few more days? Until we figure out who set Fowler up and how."

"I'm staying at the ranch until Courtney Rogers gets a replacement for me," Riley bit out. "Big Sky got her foreman to quit, and I'm not leaving a pregnant woman in the lurch."

The colonel had the grace to look embarrassed.

"You can give me a ride back," Riley said, pressing his advantage. "As soon as I take a shower."

"Okay," Murphy agreed.

"You got any clean clothes? I don't want to go back there smelling like Santa Claus on Christmas Eve."

"That can be arranged."

Forty minutes later they were on the highway, heading toward the Golden Saddle.

When they passed a lighted sign along the highway, Murphy gestured. "If you need us, we're at the Buckskin Motel. Right over there. We've rented rooms five through fifteen."

Riley didn't bother telling him it was the same motel where he'd taken Courtney that first afternoon, when he'd found her stranded beside the road. It seemed like a lifetime ago, when it was really only a few weeks.

Tension gathered inside him as they turned up the ranch road and headed for the house.

Murphy glanced at him. In a voice that was half-teasing, he asked, "How about if I tell her that you were working for me?"

"I'd rather handle it myself," Riley said as Courtney barreled out the front door, gun in hand, and stopped short when she saw the unfamiliar SUV.

"That's quite a woman you've got there. You want us to wait around—in case she shoots you?" Joseph Brown quipped from the driver's seat.

"You take care of your own woman. That princess. She's a handful, too. Right?"

That shut Brown up. But Riley still had to deal with the spitfire standing in the ranch yard with a gun. And he didn't want anyone else getting caught in the crossfire.

"You guys get the hell out of here before the rough stuff starts."

Murphy looked doubtful, but he did as Riley asked—because he owed him that much after giving him the most dangerous part of this assignment

Riley climbed out of the SUV and started toward the house, holding the arm Fowler had cut stiffly against his body and trying not to limp.

"Put the gun down," he said wearily. "If you want to shoot me, do it after my friends leave, so there won't be any witnesses." Before she could answer, he turned and waved to Brown.

After several seconds hesitation, the SUV drove off, leaving Riley wondering if Courtney was going to kick him off the ranch in the next five minutes.

She stood staring at him like she didn't believe he was real.

"Do I look that bad?" he asked.

"You look like you've been in a fight and you got the worst of the deal."

"The other guy is dead."

She sucked in a sharp breath. "You're saying you killed someone?"

"No. Unfortunately. Fowler got away from me, but Murphy and the guys tracked him into the national park. He won't be bothering you again."

"Who's Murphy?"

"Long story. But I need to sit down first."

When Riley started toward the house, Jake stepped onto the porch and gave him the evil eye. "Where do you think you're going? We don't want you around here."

"I guess that's for Ms. Rogers to decide," he answered, then gave her a questioning look.

"Go on in," she murmured.

Riley wanted to tell the guy to butt out, but he kept his head down and his mouth shut as he walked past Jake and into the house.

Apparently the old ranch hand wasn't going to leave it at that. They all ended up in the living room, where Riley sat down heavily on the sofa, then looked around in surprise. He'd been too busy to think about Christmas except for his Santa Claus remark. But while he'd been gone, someone had decked out the room for the holidays, with fresh greens on the mantel and a six-foot fir tree, decorated with beautiful handmade ornaments.

He looked from the trimmings to Courtney. "You've been busy."

"I needed to focus on something positive...." The sentence trailed off. She cleared her throat and began again. "Jake and the men helped me."

"Good idea," Riley managed, thinking that having them around her had provided extra security.

Courtney turned toward Jake. "I'd appreciate it if you'd leave us alone."

He wedged his hands on his hips. "You know I can't do that. I've got an obligation to you."

"Well, your obligation to me is to leave," she said firmly. "Don't forget you work for me, and I'm giving you an order."

"He could hurt you," Jake insisted.

"Does he look like he's in shape to hurt anyone?" she asked sharply.

Jake ran his gaze over Riley's sorry self. "I guess not," he muttered, then stomped out of the room. But he lingered in the hallway.

"I'll be fine," Courtney called out.

When they were finally alone, she turned back

to Riley and slicked her hands down her sides. "I was worried about you."

He wanted to make something of that. But it might just be a polite comment, so he cleared his throat and said, "Sorry. I came here as soon as the medics let me go."

"You were in the hospital?"

"Yeah."

"Why?"

"Smoke inhalation." He kept the knife wound to himself.

She looked as if she wanted to cross the room to him. He waited with his breath frozen in his lungs. Unfortunately, she stayed where she was.

"The fire at the women's shelter rated a special radio report," she said. "The newscaster on the scene said you saved a lot of people."

Riley gave a small nod.

"And a group of men nobody had seen around here before were also in the thick of it."

"Big Sky," Riley told her. "The outfit I work for."

"So are you still keeping the whole thing a big secret?"

"Not now. We're all former military. Colonel Cameron Murphy personally selected each of us." He drew in a breath and let it out. "We're bounty hunters."

Courtney's gaze turned hard. "And you were after Fowler?"

"Yeah. We've been pursuing him for months." He plowed ahead because he owed her an explanation. "Fowler headed up a sinister militia group that has caused unspeakable harm. He broke out of prison with a group of his cohorts, and we've been slowly rounding the fugitives up. But Fowler was the most dangerous—and elusive—of the bunch. And he made our lives a living hell. Shortly before I arrived here, he held us in captivity at his prison camp. We escaped, and he thought we all died in an explosion. But I'm good at disguising myself. The colonel figured Fowler wouldn't make me. So he sent me here."

She gave him a quizzical look. "You mean you've really got dark hair and bushy eyebrows?"

The comic picture made him bark out a laugh. "No. This is the way I normally look. When he captured us, I was carrying a false ID, and I had my hair dyed. Then he shaved my head with a dull razor, so I looked considerably different."

She winced, then her features sharpened. "It sounds like your friend, the colonel, was taking a chance—that Fowler wouldn't recognize you and kill you."

"It was an acceptable risk. And I pulled it off."

"Just like you pulled off pretending to be a ranch manager," Courtney pointed out.

Riley looked down at his hands. "I know enough to get by."

"And you think that's what I deserved?"

"If you want my answer now, it's no. Back when I came here, we couldn't tell if you rented to Fowler because you were cozy with him. And we didn't know you were pregnant."

"Oh, that makes it all right!"

"I understand why you should kick me out," Riley said, struggling to keep his voice steady. He pushed himself up, swaying on his feet. "I'll get out of your way."

He started past her, but she grabbed his arm. Caught off guard, he groaned.

She gave him a long look. "Your arm's hurt."

"It's nothing."

"Don't tell me nothing. What happened?"

"Fowler cut me. It's stitched up."

"You should lie down," she said.

"In the bunkhouse, for tonight, if you don't mind me taking my old bed back."

He waited for her answer. Waited for her to say that she was going to kick him out on his ass—into a snowbank.

Chapter Fifteen

Riley watched Courtney take her lower lip between her teeth.

"You're going to hurt yourself if you keep doing that," he whispered.

"Doing what?

"Biting your lip."

She nodded, her tongue flicking out to soothe the place where the teeth had been, and he couldn't stop his gaze from locking on the sensual movement.

"It's hard to…to…trust you," she whispered.

"I know. I came to the Golden Saddle with ulterior motives." He wanted to keep talking—to tell her how much things had changed since the colonel had sent him here. He wanted to tell her how much he cared for her. But it wasn't fair to barrage her with words. So he waited in silence.

When she finally spoke, he could hardly hear her above the ringing in his ears.

"Riley, you saved my life tonight. I'm so fat and awkward that if I'd been in that battered-women's shelter, I probably couldn't have gotten out."

"You're not fat and awkward!"

"Don't tell me how I feel!" She glared at him, and he closed his mouth.

"Let me finish. Ever since I heard the news report, I've been thinking about the way you came here earlier this evening."

"I had to warn you."

"But Fowler was expecting you to be with his men, wasn't he?"

He nodded.

"I guess you had to do some fast talking when you got back."

"Yeah."

She shuddered. "I can't believe I allowed a creep like Fowler to hole up on my property."

He squeezed her hand. "Don't be so hard on yourself. He was a master manipulator. He's the most cunning perp we've ever chased."

"I should thank you for saving my life instead of accusing you of being underhanded."

He might have said, "I'm not proud of deceiving you." But he'd learned when to keep his mouth shut.

They stood silently facing each other. Then, to his astonishment, she stepped forward and pressed her lips to his.

It was a sweet kiss, a thank-you kiss. But to him it meant so much more, and he couldn't simply stand there and let it be over in an instant.

"Oh, Courtney," he murmured, "you are everything I ever dreamed of in a woman."

She pulled back enough to study his face. "You can't mean that."

"Of course I do." His arms came up. Gently, mindful of her condition, he gathered her to him, holding her tenderly because she was precious to him and the thought of losing her was like losing part of himself.

He had already said too much about his assignment. And he wasn't free to say more. Not while they were still trying to figure out who had set up Boone Fowler and his militia men. And how.

But he hoped he could show her his feelings. He moved his lips against hers, demanding nothing, yet silently asking if she would accept more.

She told him she would by returning the kiss with a fervor that had him instantly hard as a poker.

He wanted to pull her body tightly against his. But he managed to keep his hold on her light.

She made a small sound of wanting that almost stole his sanity. If she had been any other woman, he would have torn off her clothes, pulled her down to the rug and made passionate love to her in front of the Christmas tree. But she was almost eight months pregnant, and caveman tactics were out of the question.

Still, standing had become impossible. He'd been through a hell of a lot this evening, and his knees were weak, from kissing her as much as from anything else.

When he scooped her up into his arms, she made a small sound of surprise.

The pressure hurt his injured arm, and he winced.

"Riley?"

"We're not going far," he muttered as he sat down heavily in an overstuffed chair.

Adjusting her weight, he cuddled her against him, reveling in the warmth of her body, burying his face in her hair, breathing in her wonderful scent.

The words "I love you" clamored behind his lips. He wasn't free to say them. Maybe he'd never be free to tell her. But he could kiss her and stroke her and give her pleasure.

She could have pushed herself up and put some distance between them. She could have told him he was a lying bastard who had no right to touch her like this.

But she stayed where she was, exchanging hot, wet kisses. When his fingers brushed back and forth across her breasts, joy rose inside him as he felt her hardened nipples and knew she was responding to him the way he was to her.

He couldn't stop himself from sliding his hand under her skirt and up her leg to the hot, moist core of her.

When he began working his way under the leg of her panties, she reached down and closed her fingers around his.

"Don't."

He squeezed his eyes tightly shut, struggling to remember why he had no right to touch her like that. "I'm sorry," he managed to say.

She pressed her cheek to his and spoke with her lips against his ear. "We should go back to the bedroom if we're going to continue this."

"Is that what you want?"

"Yes." She climbed awkwardly off his lap and held out her hand, looking so shy and vulnerable that his heart turned over inside his chest.

He stood and reached for her, and the words he had been trying not to say tumbled out. "Courtney, I love you."

She raised her head and looked into his eyes. "You hardly know me."

"I'm a good judge of people. I've got to be in my job. I know you well enough to see you've got grit and courage. And determination. Yet you're so soft and feminine."

"And a little naive," she added.

"Yeah. That, too."

She licked her lips. "I…can't…make any commitments when I don't know—"

He jumped in before she finished. "You don't have to say any more. Not until I prove to you that I'm not the lying rat who came to your ranch under false pretenses."

"You're not a lying rat!"

"Let's not waste time arguing," he said, his grip firming on her hand. He was the one who led them down the hall into the bedroom. He didn't know exactly what she had in mind. Maybe she was too far along now for him to do more than hold her. But he'd love to do just that. And one more thing. If he didn't see her, he would go insane. So he crossed the bathroom and turned on the light, leaving the door partly ajar.

Then he closed and locked the bedroom door—so that busybody Jake couldn't come bursting in on them…using the excuse that he thought Courtney was in danger.

She stood awkwardly in the middle of the room. "You know I feel…embarrassed about the way I look," she murmured.

"I told you. You look very sexy to me. Very feminine." As he spoke, he walked toward her and stopped inches away. Raising a hand that trembled slightly, he traced his fingers over the swell of her breasts, stroking her distended nipples before sliding his hand downward so he could circle the larger swell of her belly.

She was silent for several moments, then blurted, "You know the right things to say. You did from the beginning."

The observation stung, because it didn't simply apply to this situation. She could just as well be talking about the line he'd fed her—about his ranch manager experience.

"Is fast talking part of your training?"

"Yeah. We get a course in BS."

She laughed.

"But the things I said to you—the personal things were all true." He heaved in a breath and let it out. Because he needed to lay his cards on the table, he said, "And from now on, you can count on my being absolutely straight with you. About everything." He swallowed. "But I know it's going to take time for you to believe that."

He understood why she still couldn't completely trust him, though he was pretty sure she wanted to. And he set about helping the process along in the best way he could think of, kissing her and stroking her as he found the zipper at the back of her dress and lowered it.

He moved slowly, taking her with him and leaning against the door because he wasn't quite steady on his feet. Giving her time to object, he splayed his hands over the hot skin of her back before shifting the dress off her shoulders and lowering the front.

She was wearing a no-nonsense-looking maternity bra. He unhooked that, too, lifting it away and freeing her breasts. They were voluptuous and firm, the nipples large and dark.

She tried to cover them with her hands. But he caught her wrists.

"You are so sexy," he whispered, then lowered his head, stroking his tongue around first one nipple and then the other. He wanted to suck. But he suspected that might embarrass her. So he held the impulse in check while he lowered her dress, pulling down her half slip, too.

"I'm so big,"

"Of course not. You ought to have seen one of the women on the ranch where I grew up. She got so enormous she looked as if she'd topple over if you gave her a little push."

Courtney answered with a nervous laugh.

"You've just got a cute little potbelly."

Shifting the attention away from her, he said, "I feel like I'm a bit overdressed. Would you help me off with my clothes?"

She tackled his belt buckle while he worked the

buttons on his shirt. When he tried to shrug out of the shirt, he gritted his teeth.

"Your arm?"

"Yeah."

Working carefully, she helped him get the shirt off his shoulders, then dragged in a sharp breath when she saw the bandage covering most of the skin from his shoulder to his elbow.

"It looks worse than it feels," he said quickly.

"I think you're lying about that. How many stitches?"

"Around twenty."

"Ouch."

"I think you can help me forget about it," he countered, "if I can just get out of these damn pants."

She went back to work on his zipper. And he drew in a strangled breath when she closed her hand around his erection.

"That feels so good," she murmured.

He laughed. "I think I'm getting the better part of the deal."

He kicked off his boots and pants. Knowing he couldn't manage to stand up much longer, he led her toward the bed and pulled the covers aside so they could both slip under.

He had lain behind her last time. Now he turned her toward him, holding her tenderly as he kissed and stroked his hands over her lush body, marveling that he was in her bed again.

"Is it all right to make love with you?" he asked.

"Yes."

Thank heavens, he thought. But he didn't say it aloud. He was already balanced on a fine blade of arousal. Trying to ignore the need for release, he focused on her pleasure, stroking between her legs, over her breasts, bringing her need up to match his.

He felt her body respond, heard the breath hissing in and out of her lungs. But she said nothing.

"Courtney, are you ready for me?"

"Yes," she whispered.

"This time, when I'm inside you, will you let me see you?" he asked, holding his breath as he waited for her answer.

"Then…I'd have to be on top."

"Mmm-hmm."

His heart pounded in his chest as he watched her consider her decision. His relief surged as she moved awkwardly, coming up on her knees. He helped her straddle his body, and he looked his fill at her. But she kept her gaze downward.

"Sugar, look at me," he growled.

She raised her eyes, her face flushed, and he could see she still wasn't comfortable with his watching her.

"You are the most beautiful sight I have ever seen. And so damn sexy," he repeated.

"That's hard to believe."

"I told you—every word you hear from my lips is the honest truth."

She nodded, then began to move above him, and he fought the tide of need raging through him. As he drank in the sight of her riding him, he reached to press his fingers against the spot where her pleasure centered.

She looked down at him, her eyes heavy-lidded and sensual.

"Touch your breasts. Let me see you do that."

Her flush deepened, but she did as he asked, stroking her fingers over her generous curves and her nipples as she moved faster—her need for release overtaking her.

He felt her inner muscles contract, saw her features go taut. As her climax built, he let himself go. And they both cried out as ecstasy took them.

She folded against his sweat-slick chest, and he helped her to her side.

"Thank you," he murmured.

"No—thank you for helping me stop being so shy."

He hadn't known until that moment how exhausted he was. Eyes closed, he cradled her, going into a little fantasy about sleeping beside her every night and waking up beside her in the morning. Sharing his life with her. He'd never thought of settling down. Now he could hardly think of anything else. But he worked for Big Sky. He couldn't run out on them while things were still hanging.

And what about when they figured out who had set up Fowler? Could he leave then? Or did he have an obligation to Murphy and the men who had been through so much with him? The men who had become like his family.

He squeezed his eyes shut, then struggled to relax so that he wouldn't convey his tension to Courtney.

She got up several times during the night to use the bathroom. Each time she came back, he reached to touch her arm or her shoulder or the swell of her abdomen.

Just before dawn, as he caressed her tummy, he felt the baby kicking inside her, and his hand jumped.

She laughed softly. "I guess she surprised you."

"Yeah. She's strong. What does it feel like from inside?"

"Sometimes she wakes me up, but I like feeling her kick—knowing she's okay in there."

"It's a lot of responsibility—taking care of a kid."

"I'll manage," she said, her voice suddenly stiff.

He wanted to tell her he could help. But he wasn't free to make any plans with her. Not yet. So he reached for her hand and knitted his fingers with hers.

He slept again, then woke to delicious aromas coming from the kitchen. Pulling on his pants and shirt, he hurried down the hall.

He stopped short when he saw her, looking like an image from the fantasy he had conjured. She was standing at the stove, wearing another one of her cute little dresses under an apron.

He wanted to cross to her and take her in his arms. Instead he stood where he was and cleared his throat.

When she looked up, he said, "I was going to get up and make breakfast."

"You needed the sleep."

"So did you."

"I get uncomfortable, and I have to get out of bed. I thought I might as well fix us something to eat."

He shifted his weight from one foot to the other. "I need to tell you something."

Her shoulders tensed, and he knew that, despite the show of domesticity, she wasn't feeling any more comfortable this morning than he was himself.

"Before Big Sky dropped me off here yesterday, we were still trying to figure out how Fowler got his orders to torch the battered-women's shelter."

"Maybe it was his own idea."

"It was more like he walked into a trap."

She considered that. "I guess that must be true. I can almost feel sorry for him."

"Don't waste your sympathy on him—or his men. They were a pack of rats."

She nodded, then gestured toward the stove. "You look as if you could use a cup of coffee."

"I thought you weren't drinking it."

"I'm not. I made it for you. I guess I'm over the upset stomach phase of the pregnancy."

"I appreciated that. I mean the coffee." He poured a mugful, standing close enough to touch her. But he kept his hands wrapped around the warm ceramic because he was feeling less certain of himself in the morning. Last night had been simple. He'd needed her in his arms. This morning there was a lot more at stake. Because he couldn't deal with the personal stuff, he focused on business.

"Fowler could have thought of the attack, but he didn't. When he got to the shelter, somebody had rigged the place to go up in flames. Not the front part of the building—the back. Which leads to the conclusion that someone wanted them to go in there and get killed."

"Who?"

"Somebody ruthless." He went on quickly because the next part needed saying. "Fowler and his men were going into the shelter to shoot up the dignitaries and audience. He was going to take the first lady and some of the officials. He gave a direct order for one of his men to shoot you."

She sucked in a sharp breath. "Why are you telling me that?"

"So you'll watch your back. Like I've been trying to get you to do all along."

"Fowler is dead."

"Killing you could have been his idea. Or it could have been the people running the show. So I'd like to stay here in the house, until I know you're safe."

He watched emotions warring on her face. "I don't like thinking that someone is hunting me," she finally said.

"I know. I damn well don't like it, either." He set down the mug with a thunk and did what he'd wanted to do since he'd walked into the kitchen. Reaching out, he gathered her into his arms and held on. She stood stiffly for a moment, then melted against him, and he let out a sigh of relief.

"Let me be here for you."

"For how long?" she said in a barely audible voice.

"For as long as you need me," he answered, hearing the gritty sound of his own voice.

Her hands tightened on his arms and then released. "I…"

"You don't need to make any long-range decisions yet," he assured her when what he wanted to do was extract promises—and make them, too. "We can take this a step at a time. And the first step is to let me move into the house…so I can protect you."

She thought about that for a few moments, then answered, "Okay."

"Good. So what do we have for breakfast?" he asked, pretending that was his only concern.

"I made blueberry muffins. And a…Mexican egg soup."

"I never heard of that."

She flushed. "I got it out of a cookbook. You poach the eggs in a tomato-salsa liquid."

"Well, it sounds wonderful. Can I do anything to help you?"

"Pour orange juice, if you want some."

He poured the juice, and they sat down across from each other, like they were a married couple or something. Would she accept a guy like him as a husband? Someone who put himself in danger—like Edward Rogers? He wanted to talk about that, but he wasn't free to make any promises until the end of the assignment.

After spreading a muffin with butter, he looked up to find her fiddling with her soup spoon. "Is there something you want to talk about?"

"Yes, I was still thinking about the attack last night. I knew there was going to be a surprise guest at the women's shelter. Maybe I should have said something to you."

"You didn't know the center was going to be attacked."

She nodded.

"How did you find out about the first lady?" he wondered.

"Well, I didn't actually realize it was her. I talked to the director a few days ago. The last time we were in town."

"Uh-huh."

"She said someone important was coming. But she let me think Prince Nikolai was coming. I was looking forward to seeing him in person."

"Yeah."

She went on in a musing voice. "But the whole time I was waiting to see him, I kept thinking about how strange his language can be. Sometimes he uses double-negative or slang expressions. Or the wrong verb form."

"Yeah. We talked about that before, and I noticed it when I went to hear him. Like when he said 'we don't get no satisfaction out of the terrorists' attacks in the United States.'"

"Maybe he's imitating the Rolling Stones," Courtney said with a laugh.

Riley grinned back, glad that she'd brought a little humor into the situation.

But her remark had sent his thoughts down an interesting path. When they'd finished breakfast, he said, "I have some things to discuss with Big Sky."

"Your bounty hunter organization," she said stiffly, letting him know she was still thinking about how he'd ended up at the Golden Saddle.

"Uh-huh."

"You can use the phone in the office."

"My cell phone is better. It's a secure line."

"Right."

"But I will use the office." So much for being honest with her. Well, that wasn't it exactly. He had business to discuss, and it had to stay secret.

He went down the hall and closed the door, then punched in the number for Big Sky.

Owen Cook answered.

"I have a theory I want to discuss with you," Riley said.

"About what?"

He stopped, realizing he had a problem. This line was supposed to be secure. But the bad guys had taken everybody by surprise last night. They might do it again—with equipment that could intercept the call. And if they did, that would be disastrous. "Maybe I'd better come over there," he said.

"We'll be expecting you."

He went back to find Courtney loading the dishwasher.

"You finished so quickly?" she asked.

"Unfortunately, I figured out that I can't discuss this particular business over the phone."

"And?"

"I have to go see them."

"So much for your staying around," she whispered.

He felt his chest tighten. "I'm sorry. While we're in the middle of this situation, I don't know what else to do."

She nodded tightly.

"Until I come back, how about if Jake stays here with you?"

"I don't need a babysitter," she snapped.

"I know. But I'll feel better about being off the ranch property if I know someone you trust is with you."

"Fine!" She slapped a mug into the dishwasher.

When he started to help her, she shook her head. "I can do it. You go to your meeting."

He didn't like leaving her this way—not when she was upset with him. And not when it was his own damn fault. He shouldn't have said he would stay here when he knew he might have to go. All he could say was, "I'll move my stuff over here first."

As he started to step through the doorway, she called out, "Wait!"

He turned to face her.

"I guess my…my hormones are acting up. I'm upset, but I shouldn't have taken my anxieties out on you."

"I understand," he said.

"Go on. And take care of that business."

"You're sure?"

"Of course. Put your things in the spare bedroom," she said.

"Sure," he answered, wondering if the suggestion was for appearances' sake or if she was making it clear that her bed was off-limits from now on. He didn't have the guts to ask, so he grabbed his coat and went over to the bunkhouse.

As he was packing his things, Jake came to the bedroom door. "Leaving?"

You wish.

"I'm moving into the main house."

"Says who?"

"I want somebody around there at night until the current situation is resolved."

"Sure you do," Jake muttered.

Riley clenched his hands, but he kept his temper under control because he and Jake were already standing on shaky ground.

"I'll be going into town for a while. I'd appreciate it if you'd keep an eye on Mrs. Rogers until I get back."

"When will that be?"

"I'm not sure."

"You want me in the house with her?"

"If you can spare the time. But I think that's not absolutely necessary during the day."

"Yes, boss," Jake said with a sneer, and Riley wondered what he had to do to get on the good side of this man.

He threw his belongings into his duffel bag and took them across the ranch yard. Courtney was standing in the living room rearranging ornaments on the Christmas tree.

"I'll be back as soon as I can," he said, after dumping his possessions on the floor in the guest room.

"Okay."

She smoothed her hand down her side, pulling the dress more tightly against her belly, then must have realized what she'd done and dropped her hand.

"Where are you going—exactly?" she asked.

"It's better if I don't tell you. But you can call my cell phone if you need me." He wrote down the number on a piece of paper and set it on the end table.

"Thanks," she whispered.

He stood looking at her, then crossed the space between them and folded her into his arms. To his relief she returned the embrace, and they clung together—until he gave her one more squeeze, then eased away.

Turning, he forced himself to walk out of the room, then out of the house. He had an obligation to contact Big Sky, but as he drove away, he was still thinking about what he'd told Courtney. The bad guys could be using high technology. Or maybe there was another, much lower tech, explanation for their success. He had to discuss the possibilities with the colonel.

Still, he felt a sense of dread as he left the ranch property and headed for the motel where the men from Big Sky had taken rooms.

Murphy answered his knock.

He stepped inside and closed the door against the cold. Cook, Powell and Martin greeted him warmly.

"How's the arm?" Powell asked.

"Healing."

Murphy was watching him. "Last night you said you wanted to keep an eye on Mrs. Rogers. What took you away from the ranch?"

"I'd like to test an interesting theory." He gestured toward the laptop computer set up in one corner of the room. "Can we get copies of Prince Nikolai's speeches? Particularly the last one—a couple of days before the fire at the battered-women's shelter."

Murphy tipped his head to one side, considering the question. "You think the speech is connected to the attack?"

Riley looked at the colonel. "Mrs. Rogers and I were talking about the prince's diction. We discussed it a couple of times because it made such an impression on her. She pointed out that he was educated at Harvard, but he lapses into ungrammatical constructions when he's giving his speeches."

"And?" the colonel pressed.

"Suppose he's not just going around the country giving pep talks to our citizens. Suppose he's up to something we haven't figured out."

"Like?"

"For starters, using some kind of code."

Cook had been listening intensely to the conversation. "Let me take a look."

He sat down at the computer, called up a copy of the prince's latest speech and began doing some kind of analysis that Riley couldn't follow.

When Riley leaned over to watch, Cook rolled his shoulders. "Don't stand behind me," he muttered.

"Sorry." Riley moved away, suppressing the impulse to start pacing. He knew he wasn't going to get instant results, yet he couldn't help the feeling of restlessness that gripped him. He wanted to know what had happened last night—and why.

Murphy came up behind him. "Let's go in the other room," he suggested. "I'd like to get your impression of Sheriff Pennington."

Riley snorted. "He's a real piece of work. He was obviously in bed with the militia."

The colonel led him into the connecting room. "What did he do?"

Riley told him about his hassling Courtney—and about the way he'd deferred to Fowler after the shooting.

"Fowler also said it was the sheriff who passed on the information that the first lady was coming to the opening of the women's shelter."

"I guess the Secret Service told local law enforcement."

"A mistake on their part—since he was working with Fowler."

"Or they're both working for the terrorists."

Riley nodded. "What's he doing now?"

"Making life unpleasant for us," Clark answered from where he sat in the corner of the room.

"How?"

"Mostly asking pointed questions."

"And you're giving evasive answers."

"Right."

Murphy kept Riley busy talking about the case. When Riley heard the printer going in the other room, he looked up expectantly. Moments after it finished, Cook opened the door and walked into the room.

"What?" Riley demanded, studying the smug expression on his friend's face.

"You were right on the money," the computer expert answered. He came over and laid several sheets of paper on the table.

"Look at this. The first clue was this sentence he uses in every speech. 'Now we begin.' That leads to the question—begin what? So I started checking what he said right after that. And I noticed it's where the odd phrasing starts. See, look here. After that phrase, the first letter of every other word spoken spells out a sentence. It's not really complicated, if you know what to look for. Here's 'take your outmoded American reasoning and change the haughtiness.' If you used the first letter of every other word, you get 'torch.'"

"Cut to the chase," Riley interrupted him. "What does the whole message say."

"Torch new women's shelter. Go in back door."

Murphy swore. "All his speeches have this odd wording according to Mrs. Rogers. Well, wouldn't it be interesting if one of the prince's speeches preceded every terrorist attack."

The other men in the room had gathered around the table, looking at the message, talking excitedly.

"We thought it was King Aleksandr making trouble over here, so we'd withdraw our troops. But it looks like it was the damn prince all along," Riley spat out.

"What's his motive?" Clark asked.

"I'd guess he's been hedging his bets. If the war succeeded, then his father would be out of power—and he could take over."

The colonel jumped in, "And if terrorist acts did manage to scare the U.S. into pulling out their troops, then he'd conveniently have his father killed. And as the grieving crown prince, he would naturally take his rightful place on the throne."

Riley's eyes narrowed. "What a damn sneaky bastard. It looks like he wants his father to come across as a tyrant—so he can take over the country—either way the war turns out."

"Fowler's militia were outwardly against the war. But they were really drumming up sympathy for the prince."

They were all talking at once now, discussing the prince's cleverly twisted plans. But Riley cut to the chase. "So what do we do about it?"

"I guess we inform the feds—and they can figure out how to deal with his royal ass," Martin said. "I mean, we can hardly collect a bounty on a prince."

PRINCE NIKOLAI STOOD impatiently beside his valet as the man packed suits and shirts into his specially designed luggage. He'd given orders for his entourage to be ready to depart. Apparently Boris had taken advantage of his absence to leave the hotel on a private shopping expedition—and he'd gotten back only minutes before Nikolai.

"Hurry up," he growled. "We have a plane to catch."

"Yes, Highness," the man answered.

"Don't be so damn meticulous! Just get everything packed. Now!" he snapped.

Boris looked at him in terror, trying to cope with instructions that were the exact opposite of his usual orders.

Nikolai would punish the man later. There was no time now. With a curse, Nikolai brushed past him and grabbed a suit from its hanger. He seldom did physical labor. The squash court was his preferred form of exercise. Today he shoved the expensive garments into the packing case.

They had to be in the air before three in the afternoon. That was the deadline he'd set for himself. Maybe that had been too early. But he'd sent out the message in his speech this morning, and he was stuck with the time. Now it was imperative that he be away from this place before the last of the militia details were cleaned up.

Boone Fowler had been working for him. But the man had proved too unstable for the job. He was uncontrollable. He took on responsibility that wasn't his to take. He and his fanatical followers had paid the price for his insubordination.

The other terrorists had been much more professional. Which was why Nikolai was using them for one last job near the militia compound, to make sure Courtney Rogers couldn't tell anyone what she knew about Boone Fowler.

Meanwhile, he had to make new plans for his own future. With all the strident speeches against his father, he couldn't go back to Lukinburg until the old man was dead. But he'd struck a deal with the so-called president of one of the neighboring states. The man would take him in for "humanitarian reasons" in exchange for a large sum of money. Nikolai didn't have the cash to pay him yet, but he would get it as soon as he got his hands on the royal treasury. One way or another he was going to get his father off the throne and take over the country.

MURPHY AND HIS MEN were still discussing the prince and his underhanded tactics when Clark cut into the conversation.

"Wait a minute. Didn't he just give another speech a few hours ago?"

"Yeah," Powell answered. "I was thinking that he's been pretty active lately."

"But he can't be giving messages to the militia. They're dead."

"He could still be giving instructions to the terrorists," Riley said.

Cook hurried back to the computer and got the text of the prince's latest public appearance. This time Riley couldn't stay out of the way. He leaned over the man's shoulder, decoding along with him, his stomach knotting as the words of the message slowly emerged.

Blow up militia compound—kill Golden Saddle bitch by 3 p.m.

Chapter Sixteen

Riley felt a dagger of fear pierce his chest. When he looked at his watch, he saw it was after two-thirty.

"Oh, God, while we've been sitting around here, they've been planning to kill Courtney. We've got to get out there," he shouted, "before it's too late."

The other men were already moving, climbing into their outerwear and gathering up weapons and equipment.

When Riley pulled the door open, he saw that the weather had changed again. A swirl of snow hit him in the face.

He swore. "This is going to slow us down."

"And the bad guys, too," Cook said.

Riley muttered a response. He had already whipped out his cell phone as he trotted toward his SUV.

"Hold up. We'll go in our vehicles," Murphy

shouted. "They're faster. And they have heavy-duty snow tires."

Riley switched directions and climbed into the front seat next to the colonel. As they sped away, he punched in the ranch number. When the phone started ringing, he got ready to shout a warning as soon as Courtney answered. But the phone simply rang and rang. No answering machine. No nothing.

"I can't get through. They could already be there."

"Not likely," Murphy answered. "We'll get there in time."

Riley knew the assurance was automatic. There was no guarantee of anything. Silently he cursed himself for leaving the ranch.

"Stop beating yourself up," the colonel ordered. "If you hadn't come here with that theory about the prince, you'd have no idea that the bad guys were on their way. They would have caught her and you with your pants down."

Riley grimaced.

Murphy waited a beat, then added, "I didn't mean that literally, of course."

"Right," Riley answered, pretty sure that his commander was trying to distract him. The suspicion was confirmed by Murphy's next words.

"Use your phone to tell the feds what's going

on. They'll provide backup. And even if they get here late, they need to see what goes down at the ranch."

"Because someone could get killed," Riley clarified.

"Yeah. And it's going to be the bad guys."

In a clipped voice, Murphy gave him a direct number to the FBI regional office in Billings. But getting a simple message through wasn't easy, because the jerk who answered the phone wasn't inclined to believe the messenger. He had to confirm his identity, then wait for a decision. All of which made him want to scream.

BENDING TO THE WINDOW, Courtney peered into a sea of white. Another storm. Just when she didn't need one.

But there was more to worry about than the snowstorm. Since Riley had left, she'd been thinking about him and his friends from the bounty hunter organization. They had come here chasing down Boone Fowler. Then he'd told her the other terrorists were responsible for the death of Fowler and his men.

Were the terrorists still hanging around Spur City? If so, they were probably angry Riley and his friends had messed up their plans. Would they go after them?

Was Riley in danger?

Under ordinary circumstances, she'd call the sheriff's office. But Riley had told her Pennington was working with the militia. He could be in bed with the terrorists, too.

Her only option was to call Riley's cell phone—and hope he didn't think she was acting like a hysterical female.

With the number in one hand, she picked up the telephone receiver. If she was wrong about him being in danger, there was no harm done.

Her thoughts were racing, and she stood there holding the receiver for several seconds before she realized there was no dial tone. Had the storm knocked out the phone lines?

She walked into the living room to confer with Jake, but he wasn't there. He might have been in the bathroom, but his coat was also gone. And when she opened the front door, she saw a line of footsteps in the snow leading toward the access road.

Her brow wrinkled. What was he doing down there? Had he spotted some kind of trouble and gone to deal with it?

Unable to suppress a spurt of panic, she pulled on her coat and stepped outside, then hesitated for a moment. Her first impulse was to go after Jake. But if he'd walked into trouble, following was exactly the wrong thing to do. So she headed for the barn—where she found Billy and Kelly feeding the horses.

Her look of alarm must have given both of them the wrong idea.

"What is it?" Billy asked in a sharp voice. "Is the baby coming? Do you need to go to the hospital?"

The classic male reaction made her laugh. "No. Not that," she hastened to assure him. "Do you know where Jake went?"

"He doesn't usually tell us what he's doing," Billy said.

The strained note in his voice alerted her that something wasn't quite right. "Is that often a problem?" she asked.

Billy shrugged. "He has been disappearing a lot lately."

She looked from one man to the other. "If you were having a problem with him, you should have informed me," she said, hoping her frayed nerves hadn't made her tone too harsh.

Kelly looked down at his hands. "Yeah, well, he's been here a lot longer than we have. We figured that he had—you know—privileges."

She thought that over, then said, "Get your guns. Then come back to the house with me."

She saw Billy's Adam's apple bob. "You expecting trouble?"

She looked down the access road where Jake had taken off, wondering what he could be doing. "I hope not," she said, trying to sound like she wasn't falling apart. "But I think we'd better be prepared."

A few minutes after they were all in the house, she heard a noise outside.

Easing the blinds aside, she saw that an SUV had pulled up in the driveway. Her heart leaped when she thought it might be Riley. Still, instead of rushing toward the door, she waited a beat.

And she was glad she'd hesitated, because the scene before her eyes had her mind spinning in confusion.

Instead of Riley, Jake climbed out of the car and gestured toward the house as he stood talking to a man she didn't know.

Apparently, her trusted hand had gone down the road to meet a stranger. No, make that strangers.

More than one man had climbed out of the vehicle.

As she watched in dismay, they pulled out guns and started walking toward the house. They must be pretty confident that they had the situation under complete control.

Moving faster than she would have thought possible, she ducked away from the window and reached for the gun she kept in the drawer near the front door.

"Get down," she shouted to the two men who stood in the living room. "Before the shooting starts."

"What?" Billy asked stupidly, just as a bullet crashed into the front door.

She knew that in those old cowboy movies the actors broke out the window glass with the butts of their guns before they took a shot at anyone. But that wasn't necessary. The bullet she fired did the job very nicely.

She didn't know exactly why they were under attack. But she was gratified to see the men outside scatter.

"What's going on?" Kelly shouted.

"The bad guys showed up in the yard."

"I thought they were dead," Billy answered.

"Guess not." As she spoke, more shots crashed through another window. Thank the Lord for the stone construction. If the house had been wood, the slugs would come right through.

Feeling completely clearheaded, she shouted at Kelly and Billy, "Keep shooting. Make sure they can't get close. And turn off the lights. I'm going to get more weapons."

The men inside and the ones outside exchanged gunfire through the windows, while she managed to crawl into the den, where the locked gun cabinet was located.

She'd never thought she'd be caught in the middle of a pitched battle like this. But her father had always insisted that they should be prepared to defend themselves.

The battle raged at the front of the house while she unlocked the cabinet in the dark and got out revolvers and rifles. From the sound of the fire coming from outside, she could tell that the invaders had assault weapons. Too bad; she and her hands were no match for them. But she wasn't going to give up without a fight.

A terrible thought crossed her mind, and she went still. Were these guys just after her? What if Kelly and Billy came out with their hands up? Would that save their lives? It was a good theory, but she didn't think it held water—not when her men could act as witnesses. So, even if they'd been caught in the middle of this by accident, she didn't give them any better chance if they tried to defect.

But how long could they hold out against an assault team? And what if someone tried to sneak around the back? Or worse—what if this ended up like the battered-women's shelter? What if someone tossed a Molotov cocktail through the window?

She made her way back to the living room as

quickly as she could and handed out additional weapons and shells. "Billy," she directed, "go around to the back of the house. Don't shoot unless you see someone sneaking up on us."

He looked terrified, but she couldn't afford to have him stop functioning. "Go on," she ordered in a brisk voice. "Hurry up, before they get the drop on us."

To her vast relief, he did as she asked.

To make it look like there were still three people in the living room, she picked up another gun and began firing with her left hand as well as her right—silently thanking her father for making sure that she was almost as good a shot with either hand.

Another volley of bullets came from the front of the house, and Kelly gasped.

"You're hit," she breathed.

"Just my left arm. I can still shoot," he gasped out.

She didn't tell him to quit, but she knew that the home team wasn't going to last much longer.

Would the men out there have mercy on a pregnant woman?

She sincerely doubted it—not when they'd invaded her ranch with guns blazing.

Flattening herself against the wall, she risked a look out the window.

Shadowy figures moved through the snow, and she thought they were getting ready to rush the place.

Just then, she saw another SUV speed up the drive and skid to a halt in the snow.

Her heart leaped into her throat as more men poured out, and she figured the bad guys had called for reinforcements.

Then she saw Riley and felt her chest clench.

From the way the SUV had been moving at top speed, she figured he must have known something was up—and he'd come straight to her rescue.

"Riley, no!" she screamed, even when she knew he couldn't hear her.

But the attackers had reacted to the situation. Whirling, they started shooting at the newcomers—who returned fire.

She saw one of the invaders go down, then another. But she also saw one of Riley's friends fall to the ground.

Lord, no!

Still, it appeared that the good guys were winning. As she watched and listened, the shots were fewer and further between.

She breathed out a sigh of relief, then heard someone groan. Whirling, she saw Billy slip to the floor. He wasn't shot. He'd been knocked unconscious by a stranger—who had quietly sneaked up on them.

The man straightened, the gun pointed at her. Before he could fire, she pulled the trigger of one six-shooter, then the other, as she dodged behind an overstuffed chair.

He looked shocked as he wavered on his feet. When his gun discharged, she shot again, then again, watching with strange detachment as he hit the rug.

The front door burst open, and footsteps pounded down the hall. Riley materialized in the living room, weapon in hand, looking wildly around as he took in the situation.

Moving toward her at a dead run, he gasped out, "Courtney, are you all right?"

"Yes."

"Stay down. There may be others in here."

She did as he asked, and he ran down the hall toward the back door. She wanted to follow, but she waited with her heart pounding for him to reappear.

To her vast relief, he was back in under a minute. "All clear."

Kelly was sitting on the couch, looking dazed. Billy sat up and put his hand to his head.

Three more men came in. One knelt beside Billy. One went down the hall where the intruder had broken in. The third went to Kelly, tore his shirt away and tied a bandage around his arm.

Courtney was still lying on the floor behind the chair—with a gun in each hand.

"You can put those down now," Riley said as he moved away from Kelly.

"Oh—right." Feeling dazed and disoriented, she set down the weapons, and he did the same.

"Lord, I thought I was going to be too late," he said as he helped her up and took her in his arms. "But you held them off."

"We couldn't have done it for much longer," she answered as she allowed him to take her out of the living room and down the hall to the office.

"How did you know to bring the cavalry?" she asked.

"You gave me the clue I needed—with that comment about the prince's grammar. He was using his speeches to give orders—to Fowler and the other terrorists."

"But why? I thought he was against the war."

"And for it, too! The latest order he gave was to kill you."

She blinked. "Me? Why me?"

"It seems he considered you a loose end. Maybe because Fowler was renting from you, and he didn't want you talking about it. If that theory is correct, perhaps he was afraid that Fowler might have inadvertently dropped a clue about their unholy alliance. We'll never know for sure."

She made a strangled sound. All this time, she'd been thinking about the prince, admiring him. It had never occurred to her that he might have been aware of her, too—the owner of a small ranch in Montana. He'd thought she'd known too much and wanted her out of the way. The realization made her feel dizzy. When she wavered on her feet, Riley eased her onto the sofa across from the desk.

"It's okay. It's all over," he murmured as he turned her in his arms and held her.

"Are you all right?" he asked gently.

"I think so. Thanks to you and your friends."

"We came as soon as I knew the prince's orders."

Before they could say anything else, she heard a throat-clearing noise from the other side of the room. It was Billy. "Sorry. He got the drop on me."

"It worked out," Riley answered.

"What about Jake?" she asked. She looked down at her hands, then back at Riley. "I figured out he was working with them. Too bad I didn't realize earlier why he was so hostile to you."

"Neither one of us got it! He was acting like he was protecting you—when really he wanted me out of the way so he could operate without interference."

"Why?" she asked in a strangled voice. "Why would he turn against me?"

"He was wounded on the ground and called me over. He said he'd been here for years. And you passed him up for ranch manager. He was angry about that. Then the terrorists offered him a lot of money to keep an eye on you. It started small. Nichols would come over from the militia camp at night and Jake would give a report. But they asked more and more of him, and he didn't know how to get out of it. He couldn't tell you, and he couldn't go to the sheriff."

"How do you know all that?" Billy asked from the doorway.

"He knew he was dying, and he wanted to explain to Mrs. Rogers. The last thing he said was that he wanted her to know he wasn't in on the shooting tonight." He stopped and swallowed, looking from her to Billy and back again. "I'm sorry. He's dead." His next words were for Billy. "You go on back to the living room and sit down." The young man complied.

Emotions warred inside Courtney, but she held her voice steady as she said, "You don't have to be sorry. Not when he sold me out. Not when he told the terrorists I was alone and defenseless."

"I don't think he knew what was going to happen."

"Stop defending him." Her words had been harsh, but she found she couldn't be detached. Not when Jake had been with her for so long. "Did...did he say anything else before he died?"

"He said to tell you he was sorry."

She nodded, then asked, "Did he cut the phone wires?"

"I assume so. I tried to call you, and I couldn't get through. Who were you trying to call when you found out the phone had gone dead?"

"You. I realized you and Big Sky could be in jeopardy. And I wanted to...to make sure you were all right."

Footsteps sounded in the hall, and she tensed. A tall man with a hard-looking face and jet-black hair cut military short came into the office. She could see from the look he exchanged with Riley that they were working together.

"We have the area outside secured. Is Ms. Rogers okay?" he asked.

"Yes. We got here in time." He inclined his head toward her. "Courtney Rogers, this is Colonel Cameron Murphy."

"I'm pleased to meet you. It seems I owe you a debt of gratitude," she said.

"As soon as Watson knew you were in danger he went berserk."

"I wouldn't put it that way!" Riley objected.

"Well, you got us on the road with lightning speed," Murphy answered.

She looked at Riley. "Thank you."

He clenched his fists. "I should have stayed to make sure you were safe."

"Then you wouldn't have known about the code in the prince's speeches," the other man reminded him.

The sound of more vehicles arriving in the ranch yard made Courtney's chest go tight.

When the men turned toward the front of the house, she asked, "Who is that?"

"It should be the FBI. I want them to see exactly what went down here," Murphy explained. "And I want to arrange for transportation to the hospital for Cook."

"And my ranch hands," she added, then tipped her head up at Colonel Murphy. "I'm so sorry people got hurt."

"Part of the job." He gave Riley a pointed look, then strode to the door.

"What's that look supposed to mean?" she asked.

"That he doesn't want you to see a bunch of dead bodies in the ranch yard," Riley answered. "And after the authorities photograph the dead man in the living room, Big Sky can do some cleaning up. You didn't want that old rug, did you?"

She made a raw sound. "I killed a man," she breathed, focusing on the implications for the first time.

"Self-defense," he clipped out.

She managed a small nod.

"I'm going out to the shed to get some plywood—to put over the broken windows to keep the cold and snow out," Riley said.

"Yes, thanks," she answered. She didn't want to be alone, but she knew he had work to do.

"We'll clean up the broken glass. And later we'll go over to the militia camp. My guess is that they came to kill you before blowing up the camp. So there will be evidence over there."

Until that moment, she'd forgotten all about the damage from the battle. Lord, her house must be a mess. Was the Christmas tree all right? She fought to hold back a strangled laugh. The Christmas tree was the least of her worries.

She sat in the office, listening to the sound of tinkling glass and then hammering. Pulling herself together, she went back to the living room and was relieved to see the body gone. So she fell back on work. As she began to sweep up broken ornaments, one of the Big Sky men held a dustpan for her.

She worked automatically, keeping her focus on the task. But when she saw a stranger in the doorway, her head jerked up.

"Yes?"

A man walked toward her, holding out a badge. "Special Agent Paul Stanton, ma'am. I need to ask you some questions."

"Yes, of course."

He took her through an account of the invasion, then went back outside.

Alone again, she sat in the office, waiting for everyone to clear out of the house. Riley was outside conferring with the men from Big Sky and the federal agents.

When he came back, the colonel was with him.

"We're all done here, ma'am," he said. "The translation of the code from the prince's speeches should be enough to get him in big trouble."

"Will he be arrested?"

"We don't know yet."

Riley broke into the conversation, his voice soft. "Billy and Kelly have already left in an ambulance. Big Sky is leaving, before they get snowed in."

"It's that bad outside?" she murmured. She hadn't thought of the snow for hours.

"Your hands will get back here as soon as they can. Meanwhile, I'll take care of the ranch."

"Yes. Thanks," she answered, wondering what was going to happen after that.

"You try to get some rest," he said, then went back outside.

RILEY STOPPED in the ranch yard with the colonel.

"I'd offer to deliver your car out here in the morning," Murphy said. "But I'm not sure the roads will be passable."

Riley nodded. "We'll play it by ear."

He watched his friends leave, thinking he didn't know what the future held. But he knew there was farm work to do. The horses needed to be fed. And the stalls mucked out.

Mechanically, he took care of the chores, knowing that he had to talk to Courtney, and wondering what she was going to say to him, because until he settled things with her, he had no idea what to tell the colonel.

By the time he came back to the house, he was struggling through eighteen inches of snow. And the damn storm showed no signs of abating.

He should shovel a path to the barn. But after the gun battle and the aftermath, he was bone tired. And anything he cleared away out here would just get buried again. So he might as well wait until the morning.

With that rationalization in place, he staggered into the house. It was almost a relief to find that Courtney had gone to bed.

In the spare bedroom, he grabbed clean clothes and took a shower, standing under the hot water for a long time, letting the warmth sink into his bones.

Then he pulled on a long-sleeved shirt and sweatpants and fell into bed, thinking how crazy he'd been to entertain any fantasies about Courtney Rogers. What did he think—that she was going to invite him to share an expensive piece of property like the Golden Saddle Ranch?

He lay awake chewing on that for a long time. But finally he slept.

His eyes blinked open when he heard Courtney calling to him. She was standing in the doorway to the bedroom, dressed in a long flannel gown, the light from the hallway streaming in behind her.

"Riley, I'm sorry to wake you up."

He heard fear in her voice. Sitting up, he grabbed the gun he'd left on the bedside table and hurried toward her.

Chapter Seventeen

"What is it? What's wrong?" Riley asked.

"You can put the gun down. There's nobody here besides us."

Confused, he tried to bring the situation into focus. "What do you need?" he asked.

"I know it's a month early. But…but…I woke up, and I'm having contractions. I…I need to get to the hospital. I guess the excitement of the gun battle…" Her voice trailed off on a gasp of pain.

"Oh, Lord." He slung his arm around her, pulling her against his side and helped her to the bed. "You'd better sit down."

She closed her fingers around his arm. "You don't understand," she said, making every word distinct and clear. "I have to get to the hospital."

He felt like the bottom had just dropped out of his stomach. But he struggled to keep the sudden panic from showing on his face. In a voice that felt detached from his vocal cords, he said, "Courtney, we're not going anywhere. I mean, leaving the house would be dangerous—for you and the baby. There's two feet of snow out there. If we tried to drive, we could get stuck."

"No," she said, then clutched his arm and gasped.

It took several moments before she dragged in a breath and said, "They're getting worse. When I first woke up, I thought…I was hoping that they were…you know, Braxton Hicks."

"What's that?"

"Just false contractions. I mean, they don't mean you're going into labor. But these haven't stopped. They're getting closer together…and harder."

"Okay. I'll take care of you…"

"Riley…you're not a doctor."

"I'm not a vet, either. But I knew what to do for Buttercup." He hoped that was reassuring to her. At least the recent memory helped him.

Mentally, he was trying to summon up everything he'd ever learned about childbirth. Long ago, when he'd been a kid on the ranch, a couple of women had given birth at home. He'd been fascinated, and he'd listened wide-eyed to the women talking about what they needed to do.

"You lie down," he said. "I'll be right back."

"Where are you going?" she asked, her voice edged with alarm.

"To boil water. They always boil water, right?" he asked, wondering if he sounded like he was babbling. "And…to get some extra bedding. Do you have a plastic sheet?"

"No. But I've got plastic tablecloths. In the buffet in the dining room. And…and I was always afraid I might be stuck in a snowstorm. So I packed a kit of stuff I might need. It's in the front hall closet."

"Good. I'll be right back. You hold tight."

She lay back on the bed and closed her eyes while he hurried down the hall and snatched up the phone in the kitchen, then cursed when he remembered that bastard Jake had cut the damn lines. When he opened the front door and looked out to assess the weather conditions, a blast of cold air and snow hit him in the face.

In the hall, he reached for his coat and fumbled in the pockets—praying that the mobile phone would work.

Swiftly he punched in the number for Big Sky. It took several rings before the colonel answered. "It's two in the morning," he growled. "This better be good."

"I need help."

The terror in his voice must have gotten Murphy's attention. "Are you under attack again? What?"

"Courtney's in labor. The baby is a month early. And I suspect the roads are impassable. Is there any chance of getting help? The baby may need medical attention."

"Just a minute."

He heard fumbling sounds and low voices on the other end of the line. Then the colonel came back on. "I'd send a chopper. But they can't take off and land. The wind is too high."

Riley cursed.

"We may be able to reach you in a snowcat."

"Yeah, and maybe you can pick up a doctor on the way."

"Riley!" Courtney's voice, high and sharp, reached him from the bedroom.

"She's calling me. I gotta go. If you can get here, I'd be grateful."

He hung up, found the tablecloth and ran back down the hall to the spare bedroom.

Courtney was leaning back against the pillow, obviously in pain.

"Oh, sugar," she gasped.

When the contraction eased, he said, "A bad one?"

"Yes," she gulped. "And only two minutes from the last one. I think it's going to be soon."

"Okay. Let's get ready."

He turned to the closet and pulled out a man's

flannel shirt. "I think you'll be more comfortable in this than that long gown."

"Yes. And…and I want to go to the bathroom."

While she was gone, he got the kit she'd prepared and checked the contents, then looked up as she came back, wearing the shirt and a look of terror.

He'd gotten the bed ready and set out supplies. The water on the stove would be boiling soon. He could use it to sterilize the scissors to cut the baby's cord.

"My water broke."

"Good. That's good," he said, wondering if it should have happened now. Or later.

After helping her onto the bed, he reached for her hand. When she clamped his fingers in a death grip, he knew another contraction had grabbed her.

As it eased, she whispered, "I'm scared."

He wanted to say the same thing. He was scared spitless. But he had to project every ounce of strength he could muster. So he simply said, "We'll get through this—together."

"Okay."

She lay with her eyes closed for several moments, holding on to him, then turned her face toward him and opened her eyes. "Riley, after the attack—why didn't you come back to bed with me?"

That was the last thing he'd expected her to say. And his answer came out in a shallow breath. "You told me to put my things in the guest bedroom. I wasn't sure you wanted me in bed with you."

"I did. That was just—you know—for appearances' sake." She heaved a sigh. "I'm sorry you're stuck in this situation."

"I'm not stuck. I'm glad I'm here to help you."

He saw her take her bottom lip between her teeth.

"I told you not to do that. You'll hurt your lip."

She nodded, then asked in a barely audible whisper, "In the morning, were you going to tell me you were leaving?"

He swallowed. He'd vowed to speak only the truth. But it was hard to say. "No. I was wondering if you...if you could love a guy like me."

Her grip tightened on his hand. "Yes. Yes I could. But I wouldn't try to hold you here. Not if you wanted to leave and go back to Big Sky."

"So each of us was thinking the other...might back away?" he managed.

Her eyes were bright. "It looks like it."

"Courtney, you've made me want all the things I thought I'd never have. A wife. A home. A family."

She started to speak. Then her hand clamped on to his in a death grip, and he knew she was in pain.

He ached to take the pain away, but all he could do was cling to her hand.

When the contraction was over, she gasped, "I feel like I have to push."

It was all happening too fast. He wasn't ready. But he wasn't going to let her down.

"Okay, I've got to wash my hands. I'll be right back." He dashed into the bathroom and washed.

Her head was turned toward the door, watching for him as he strode back into the room.

He helped her down to the end of the bed, then swept her shirt out of the way and leaned over, wishing there was more he could do as she pushed with another contraction.

"I can see the baby's head," he breathed. "You're doing fine. Perfect."

It was strange to hear his own voice sounding so calm and controlled when his insides were tied in knots. But she needed his strength, and he would give it to her.

The next contraction grabbed her, and she moaned in pain as she pushed. "Sugar! Oh, sugar!"

"Say something stronger if it helps!"

The next contraction followed hard on the heels of the last.

She was beyond answering, beyond anything but following the dictates of her body.

"Good. Perfect," he praised her. "It can't be much longer now. Everything is fine."

She bore down again, groaning with the effort.

"Her head is out," Riley told her, then sucked in a sharp breath.

"What? What's wrong?" she gasped.

"The cord is caught around her neck, but I'll get it off." He moved then, working quickly, smoothly, pulling the loop away from the baby's neck

"Riley? For Lord's sake, Riley, tell me what's happening."

"It's okay. Everything is okay. I've got it off of her," he answered, then helped deliver the baby's shoulders.

"Is she all right? Tell me she's all right," Courtney sobbed out.

Riley worked over the infant, suctioning her mouth with a syringe from the kit Courtney had put together.

When she started to cry, he felt like a lead weight had been lifted off his own chest. Laying the baby on Courtney's abdomen, he went to get the scissors from the kitchen. He also turned up the heat in the house so mother and baby would be nice and warm.

When he came back, Courtney was cuddling her child. He reached to cradle the baby's head, and Courtney's hand came up to cover his.

The power of the moment seized him, and he

blinked back tears, silently thanking God that he'd been here for her.

"Thank you," she whispered.

"I'm glad I was here."

"Yes."

There were still things to do. He helped her deliver the placenta, then cut and tied the cord. Next he washed the baby and wrapped her in one of the blankets Courtney had bought.

The infant was small, but she looked healthy— at least as far as he could tell.

"You should nurse her. That will help your uterus contract," he murmured.

"How do you know?"

He flushed. "When I was a kid, sometimes I used to eavesdrop on the women at the ranch. I was fascinated by their talk about having babies."

"I'll bet you were." She unbuttoned her shirt and put the baby to her breast, and he watched in wonder as the little girl rooted around, then clamped on to a nipple.

"Oh!" Courtney exclaimed.

She relaxed back against the pillows, and he slipped onto the bed beside her.

"You look worn-out."

"Gee, thanks."

"But beautiful."

She grinned, then snuggled against him, and he

couldn't believe he was in the middle of this sweet scene.

"Did you pick a name for her?" he asked, as he watched the small mouth working.

Courtney looked up at him, her eyes large and luminous. "I was thinking of Hannah. Or Emily. I couldn't decide which. Which do you like?" she asked in a soft voice.

"That's your decision."

"You delivered her. I'd like it to be our decision," she murmured.

He was stunned, and honored by the responsibility she'd just given him. "Hannah. I like Hannah a lot."

"It's a good name." She stroked the baby's cheek. "Hannah."

A noise outside intruded on the scene.

Courtney went rigid. "What's that?"

"Big Sky. I called them on my cell phone."

He hurried down the hall to the front door. Clark and the colonel stepped inside. Another man was with him.

"This is Dr. Rivers. He's relocating to the area. He was staying at the same motel as we were, and he volunteered to come with me."

"Thank you," Riley said simply.

He waited while the doctor checked out the baby and Courtney.

"I've got a bulletin on the prince," Murphy said with a grin.

"Oh, yeah?"

"He was on his way out of the country. But the snowstorm kept his private plane from taking off. Even when he threatened to shoot the pilot if he didn't get him out of Montana, the man wouldn't take the plane up."

"I would have liked to see that scene."

"We'd transmitted the information about the codes in Nikolai's speeches to the feds. Those bulletins were enough to get him detained for questioning."

"Good deal," Riley crowed.

In the next moment the doctor came out, and Riley went still. "How are Courtney and the baby?" he asked.

"In excellent shape. Thanks to you. The baby's heart rate and breathing are normal. Her muscle tone is good. We could transport them to the hospital, but I think they'll be more comfortable here. The roads will be clear by the afternoon. I can send a nurse out to check on them. And your wife should see her own doctor in the next few days."

Riley and the colonel exchanged glances, but neither of them corrected the doctor about the wife part.

"Appreciate it," Riley answered.

"We'll bring your ranch hands out tomorrow, so you'll have some help," Murphy said.

"Great!"

"And one more thing. We'd like…your wife… to share in the bounty on the terrorists. She earned it."

"Thanks," Riley answered, knowing that the money was going to come in handy.

After the men had left, he went back to see Courtney. The baby was in the cradle that Riley had brought into the room. And Courtney was dozing, but her eyes fluttered open and focused on him.

"The doctor says you're doing fine," he said.

"Thanks to you." She looked up at him, then stretched out her hand in invitation, and he eased down beside her.

"We were in the middle of a conversation—before Hannah interrupted us," she said.

He blinked. "What conversation?"

"The one where I was asking if you wanted to stay here at the ranch."

He felt his throat tighten. "Oh, yeah. That conversation."

"And?"

Again, only the truth came tumbling from his lips. "I'd love that."

"Edward could never adjust to ranch life," she said softly.

"Well, the ranch is perfect for me." He gathered her gently in his arms. "And so are you. I love you. And in case I haven't told you, you were pretty damn impressive—holding off a slew of armed men."

"I didn't do it alone." She kept her gaze on him. "Usually, the ranch is a lot less exciting than being a bounty hunter."

Overwhelmed with emotion, he stroked his lips against her cheek. "When I got to know you, I realized living here was what I wanted. But I was afraid to hope for—" He stopped and closed his eyes for a moment. "Does 'afraid to hope for my heart's desire' sound too…dumb?"

"Dumb? No. It sounds wonderfully poetic. You don't have to be afraid to show your poetic side with me."

"I didn't know I had one. All I know is that it seems like a dream—a wife and a daughter."

"Well, it's like that for me, too. I fell in love with you. But I fought it. I thought you'd never want to stay."

"Well, I do."

"So you're asking me to marry you?" she asked softly.

"Oh, yeah."

"I thought I'd be raising Hannah alone. I never thought I'd find love again. And now I have you."

Tears welled up in her eyes, and he tenderly brushed them away. After cuddling her for long moments, he cleared his throat.

"On a practical note, I'm due a lot of back pay. And the colonel wants you to share the bounty for Fowler and his men. That should help with the bottom line."

"I feel so blessed."

"As soon as you're on your feet, we'll get married," he murmured. "And we'll include Hannah in the wedding pictures."

She laughed. "That will be unusual."

"But a good way to start our marriage, don't you think? With the two of us and our little girl."

"Our girl," she repeated.

"Yes. If it's all right, I'd like my name on her birth certificate."

"Yes."

"And I'll have her on a horse before she's a month old."

"You're kidding."

He laughed, feeling better than he had in a long time. "Well, depending on the weather, of course. And I don't expect her to sit astride so young. I'll have her in a carrier on my back."

Courtney stared at him. "You're not kidding, are you?"

"Nope." He hugged the woman he loved and

closed his eyes, thinking he had stumbled onto everything he'd ever wanted when he'd stopped to help a stranded motorist. He hadn't known it at the time. He knew it now.

Epilogue

As Riley looked around the rustic environment of Big Sky's temporary headquarters, he felt his stomach clench.

He'd just dropped a bombshell in Cameron Murphy's lap. And he was waiting for the fallout.

"So this isn't just paternity leave?" the colonel asked.

Riley wedged his hands into his pockets, then launched into the speech he'd been rehearsing on his way here from the Golden Saddle.

"I've thought it out carefully. Courtney and the baby need me. Edward Rogers was away on foreign assignments more often than he was home. Then he got himself killed in Lukinburg. My wife needs stability—and a husband she can count on. Which means I need to stay at the ranch."

"I hate to lose a good man. But I understand," the colonel answered. "And, truthfully, I was prepared to hear you say you were leaving us."

Riley nodded. "I'm glad it's not too much of a shock."

They talked in the colonel's private office, then joined the other men in the lounge. As they stepped through the door, Riley could hear some of the others ribbing Joseph Brown about his full-blown romance with Princess Veronika. She'd been mortified to find out her brother's role in the terrorist attacks. But her former bodyguard had made her understand that her brother's dishonorable actions had nothing to do with her. After several weeks of helping her come to terms with her changed family situation, he'd gotten up the courage to ask her to stay in the U.S.—as his wife. For answer, she'd thrown her arms around his neck and kissed him.

Or so the story went. Riley was pretty sure it was a slight exaggeration. But wedding bells were definitely in the offing.

And many of the other guys were also making plans to get married to the women they'd met on this assignment.

Riley had beat them to the punch, because he'd wanted the world—particularly the upstanding citizens of Spur City—to know that Courtney and Hannah were his.

He was settling into married life at the Golden Saddle.

With Courtney's approval, they'd invited his mom up from Texas to meet his new wife and help with the baby. She and Courtney had hit it off really well. And they were thinking about making the arrangement permanent.

They'd also hired two new hands—to replace Jake and give them some extra help.

But there were still a few more loose ends he had come to discuss with Big Sky.

He told the other guys he was leaving. They were disappointed. But like the colonel, they weren't surprised.

Then they got into a discussion about Sheriff Bobby Pennington. The lawman had cut and run after the terrorists bit the dust at the Golden Saddle Ranch. And Big Sky had scooped him up. He was being held for questioning under the Patriot Act. Which meant he wasn't going to surface anytime soon.

"I hate being out of the loop. What about the prince?" Riley asked.

"He's still in custody. Even if the feds can't make a case against him stick, he's got nowhere to go. He was going to pay the president of a nearby country to take him in. But now he's barely got enough money to pay a lawyer," Cook said. His arm was still in a sling from the night of the shootout. But he was on the mend.

Riley snorted. "Good."

"Since his father's government fell and elections are scheduled, it looks like democracy is coming to Lukinburg," Murphy added.

"Yeah, I know the king went under. I wasn't sure how fast they could get a democratic government going."

"There's always been opposition to the king. Once he was out of the way, their exiled leader, Constantine Kirilovich, was able to come back. And the people have rallied around him," Murphy related.

"Good."

"I guess you haven't been keeping up with the news."

"I've been a little busy."

"Yeah. I can imagine," the colonel said.

He was about to add something more when the phone rang.

Cook picked it up, and they could tell from the expression on his face that he was blown away by whoever was on the other end of the line.

"You're not kidding, right?" he said.

The colonel pushed the speaker button, and a familiar voice boomed out. "No. This really is the president of the United States."

A hush fell around the room.

Without missing a beat, their commander an

swered, "This is Colonel Cameron Murphy. What can we do for you, Mr. President?"

"I've just been informed of the role you played in saving my wife's life—and in taking down the terrorists working with Prince Nikolai of Lukinburg. You did what the FBI and the Secret Service couldn't do. And I'm forever in your debt for saving the first lady."

"We were just doing our jobs," Murphy answered, looking around the group and giving a thumbs-up sign.

"Well, the U.S. Government offered a special reward for information leading to the capture of the men responsible for the attack on my wife. You and your men will get that, of course."

The men in the room grinned at each other.

The president cleared his throat. "I'm so impressed with Big Sky that I'd like you to consider heading up a special branch of homeland security."

Even the colonel blinked when he heard that.

"What exactly did you have in mind?" he asked.

"I'm thinking of a…special task force that goes beyond the law to protect the U.S."

"I'd need to hear more details," Murphy answered.

"Of course. And we can discuss them at a later

date. Right now I know you and your men are due for some R&R."

"Yes, sir. Can we get back to you in the next few weeks?"

"Of course."

The colonel hung up, and everyone sat in stunned silence.

"Well, how do you like them apples," Clark quipped.

"Sweet," Riley answered. "The money will be appreciated, and the job offer sounded like a wonderful opportunity for Big Sky."

"Can we tempt you back?" Murphy asked.

"Afraid not," he said without hesitation.

He had a new life now, and not even a call from the president of the United States was going to pry him away from the happiness of his new life at the Golden Saddle.

"So are we taking the commander in chief's offer?" Powell asked.

"Like I told him, we need to think about it. I suggest we don't make any decisions until we're fit and rested." He looked around the room. "And now that Watson's with us, I want to add my thanks to the president's. He saw the end result. He didn't know what we'd gone through to get here."

There were murmurs of agreement around the room.

"I knew when I assembled this group of men

we could do extraordinary things. You've all proved it in spades. And wherever we go from here—I know we'll make the right decision."

Riley felt choked up. And he knew from the expressions on the other men's faces that their emotions were running high.

Walking away from them was going to leave a hole in his heart. Yet he knew he would fill that void with the love he gave Courtney and Hannah—and the love he got back from them. His new life was already different from his old. And while he'd miss his comrades in Big Sky, he had never looked forward to the future with such joy and optimism.

Life was good.

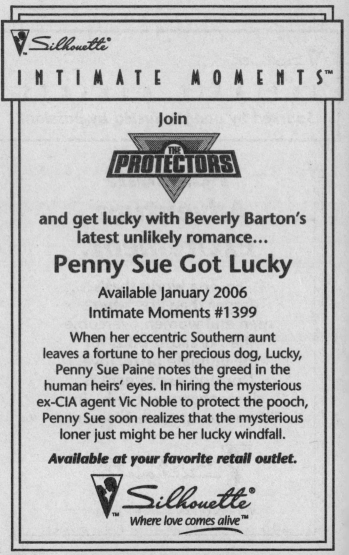

eHARLEQUIN.com

The Ultimate Destination for Women's Fiction
The ultimate destination for women's fiction.
Visit eHarlequin.com today!

GREAT BOOKS:
- We've got something for everyone—and at great low prices!
- Choose from new releases, backlist favorites, Themed Collections and preview upcoming books, too.
- Favorite authors: Debbie Macomber, Diana Palmer, Susan Wiggs and more!

EASY SHOPPING:
- Choose our convenient "bill me" option. No credit card required!
- Easy, secure, 24-hour shopping from the comfort of your own home.
- Sign-up for free membership and get $4 off your first purchase.
- Exclusive online offers: FREE books, bargain outlet savings, hot deals.

EXCLUSIVE FEATURES:
- Try Book Matcher—finding your favorite read has never been easier!
- Save & redeem Bonus Bucks.
- Another reason to love Fridays— Free Book Fridays!

Shop online
at www.eHarlequin.com today!

INTBB204R

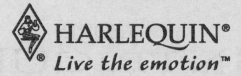
HARLEQUIN®
Live the emotion™

AMERICAN *Romance*® — Upbeat, All-American Romances

flipside — Romantic Comedy

Harlequin Historicals® — Historical, Romantic Adventure

INTRIGUE — Romantic Suspense

HARLEQUIN ROMANCE® — The essence of modern romance

HARLEQUIN® *Presents* — Seduction and passion guaranteed

HARLEQUIN Super ROMANCE® — Emotional, Exciting, Unexpected

Temptation — Sassy, Sexy, Seductive!

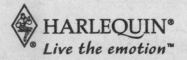